About the author

Sharon Booth writes cont
paranormal romantic comedies. Happy endings are guaranteed for her main characters, though she likes to make them work for it.

Sharon is a member of the Society of Authors and the Romantic Novelists' Association, and an Authorpreneur member of the Alliance of Independent Authors. She has been a KDP All-Star Author on several occasions.

She loves watching Doctor Who and Cary Grant movies, adores horses and hares, and enjoys strolling around harbours and old buildings. Take her to a castle, an abbey, or a stately home and she'll be happy for hours. She admits to being shamefully prone to crushes on fictional heroes.

Her stories of romance, community, family and friendship are set in pretty villages and quirky market towns, by the sea or in the countryside. Sometimes they feature ordinary men and women, sometimes they feature witches or other magical beings.

If you love heroes and heroines who are flawed but kind, who do the best they can no matter what sort of challenges they face, you'll love Sharon's books.

Books by Sharon Booth

There Must Be an Angel
A Kiss from a Rose
Once Upon a Long Ago
The Whole of the Moon

Summer Secrets at Wildflower Farm
Summer Wedding at Wildflower Farm

Resisting Mr Rochester
Saving Mr Scrooge

Baxter's Christmas Wish
The Other Side of Christmas
Christmas with Cary

New Doctor at Chestnut House
Christmas at the Country Practice
Fresh Starts at Folly Farm
A Merry Bramblewick Christmas
Summer at the Country Practice
Christmas at Cuckoo Nest Cottage

Belle, Book and Candle
My Favourite Witch
To Catch a Witch
Will of the Witch

How the Other Half Lives: Part One: At Home
How the Other Half Lives: Part Two: On Holiday
How the Other Half Lives: Part Three: At Christmas

Winter Wishes at The White Hart Inn

The Other Side of Christmas

SHARON BOOTH

Copyright © 2019 Sharon Booth.

Paperback published 2022
Cover design by Green Ginger Publishing

The moral rights of the author have been asserted.
All rights reserved. No part of this publication may be reproduced, stored in any retrieval system, or transmitted in any form, or by any means electronic, mechanical, photocopying, recording or otherwise, without the prior written permission of the publishers.

This book is a work of fiction. Names, characters, businesses, organisations, places and events other than those clearly in the public domain, are either the product of the author's imagination or are used fictitiously. Any resemblances to actual persons, living or dead, is entirely coincidental.

ISBN: 9798360418474

For anyone who's ever been alone for Christmas.

Chapter 1
It's Beginning to Look a Lot Like Christmas

It was snowing.

Why do people get so worked up about that? All afternoon customers had been coming into the shop and announcing the fact as if we were incapable of looking out of a window and seeing for ourselves.

'Blowing a blizzard out there,' they told us cheerfully. 'It'll be murder on the roads. Hope you haven't got far to go when you finish here.'

The card shop, Special Occasions, where I worked, was a hive of activity that afternoon. It never ceased to amaze me that people were still hurrying in to buy last-minute Christmas cards and wrapping paper on Christmas Eve; it's not as if Christmas sneaked up without warning, is it? How disorganised was that, for goodness' sake?

I'd signed and sealed all my cards and wrapped everything up weeks before, and not just because I work in a card shop. It's in my genes. My mum always has Christmas preparations completed by August. She buys her cards and wrapping paper in the January sales, and not from Special Occasions either. She says it's too expensive. So much for family loyalty.

Mind you, I must admit she has a point. If it wasn't for staff discount I'd probably stock up at the supermarket myself; although I still think it's worth a visit to the shop, if only to take in the festive atmosphere. With its rows of cheery cards, racks of shiny wrapping paper and shelves full of cuddly Santas and furry reindeer, it's a happy place to work. Well, most years. This year, unfortunately, the festive spirit seemed to have deserted me, and for good reason.

Even the snow wasn't lifting my mood, although I had to smile as a couple of young children stared out of the window, their eyes like saucers as they watched the big fat flakes, stark white against the dark sky, showering onto the pavement, as if someone was shaking a giant box of washing powder onto the world.

I'd just served my last customer when Penny appeared at my side ready to leave. Her hazel eyes shone with undisguised excitement as she pulled a woollen hat over her auburn curls and beamed at me. 'Hurry up, Katy. Let's get out of here. Lucy and May are practically out of the door already,' she added, nodding over to where our fellow shop assistants were hurriedly buttoning their coats and glancing nervously at the door behind the counter, as if expecting our manager to come charging through from the staff room to order them to work late.

I couldn't really blame them for wanting to get away as quickly as possible. They'd drawn the short straw. It was their turn to come in on Boxing Day, whereas Penny and I had a full two days off — although we'd done our time last year.

'Can you believe it's snowing?' Penny continued, gazing rapturously out of the window. 'That never happens on Christmas Eve does it? Who'd have thought it?'

You know what? I'd have put money on it. The one year when Christmas was a total washout from my point of view, when I'd made up my mind to ignore it to the best of my ability, it was bound to go all Charles Dickens on me. I believe it's what they call Sod's Law.

'Thank God that's over with,' she said, as I headed into the little room behind the shop and collected my coat. 'So glad it's a four o'clock finish today. Why are you dawdling? Have you forgotten it's Christmas Eve?'

'Never! Is it really? No one mentioned it.' I pulled on my gloves and wound my scarf around my neck, appalled with myself as tears suddenly appeared from nowhere. How embarrassing. I blinked them away angrily and pulled myself together. I'd be thirty in a few months, for God's sake. *Bloody hell, Katy, grow up. You can deal with this. It's just one day, after all.*

'What time are your mum and dad expecting you?' Penny called, as I hurried back into the shop, just in time to catch her in the act of popping the last chocolate into her mouth. Honestly! You'd never think that the manager had bought them for *all* the staff. Penny had demolished practically the entire box — something that clearly hadn't gone unnoticed by Lucy who tutted loudly and rolled her eyes.

'I told them to expect me when they see me,' I said, pretending not to notice her blushes because I'm nice like that. 'It's all very informal at our house. Dad will probably be asleep in front of the telly and Mum will be in the kitchen, helping herself to the advocaat and peeling three tons of potatoes. I don't have to clock on or anything.'

I could picture the scene all too clearly. It was so familiar to me, something I'd taken for granted for years. Oh heck, I was getting tearful again.

Fortunately, Penny didn't seem to notice the lack of enthusiasm in my voice. 'Lucky you,' she said, sounding gloomy. 'It's going to be manic at ours tonight when the hordes arrive. How we're going to fit everyone in I don't know. Are you sure you don't mind Mike's mum taking your room?'

'It's hardly my room,' I pointed out. 'I've only been lodging there for a few weeks. Anyway, don't be so daft; you've had this arranged for months. Oh, and don't worry, I've hidden anything that may shock her.'

Penny's eyes widened and I grinned. 'I'm kidding. Stop worrying.'

'I just feel mean,' she said. 'It would have been lovely to have you for Christmas but there just isn't the space for everyone. Mike's sister and brother-in-law will be in sleeping bags on the floor as it is.'

'You'll manage,' I said, not doubting it for a minute. Penny and Mike went through the same performance every year. Their house was invariably noisy and messy and bursting at the seams with guests on Christmas Day, but they always enjoyed it and invited everyone back for a repeat performance.

I could hardly complain about the inconvenience. They'd been good enough to take me in and let me live in their spare room for the last seven weeks. The least I could do was make way for their guests without making them feel guilty about it.

Kerry, our manager, came through to wish the four of us a merry Christmas.

'Are you sure you don't mind us leaving you to it?' I asked, feeling a bit mean.

She laughed. 'Don't be daft. Not much to do, and I've got Matt to help me.'

We all exchanged knowing looks. Matt was the assistant manager, and if he and Kerry honestly believed that none of the staff were aware of their so-called secret romance then they were seriously deluded.

Matt wandered up behind the counter and hugged us.

'We feel so bad leaving you,' May said, her voice deceptively innocent. 'It seems wrong, just the two of you, all alone in the shop.'

We avoided looking at each other as Matt held up his hands and assured us they'd be just fine. 'Get yourselves home and start partying. I shouldn't think we'll be busy for this last hour anyway. If people haven't bought their Christmas cards by now it's a bit bloody late to be worrying isn't it?'

Hiding our grins, we thanked them yet again for their cards and gifts, said goodbye and wished them a merry Christmas then headed out of Special Occasions into an alien, white world. Lucy and May hugged us then hurried off to Lucy's car, as Lucy was giving May a lift home.

A silver Astra was parked in front of the door and Penny beamed as Mike wound down his window and whistled at her. Stocky, fair-haired, and twinkly eyed, he could always be relied upon to get into the Christmas spirit, and today was no exception. He was wearing a Santa hat on his head, and I could hear Wham's Last Christmas blaring out for what felt like the thousandth time that week.

'Bloody hell, he's actually on time. It really is Christmas,' Penny said. She hugged me and told me to have a fabulous time, then climbed into the passenger seat.

'Happy Christmas,' called Mike. 'Think of us when you're lounging around stuffing your face and watching telly in total peace. I'll be putting a doll's house together, trying to fathom out my mother's new phone and watching sodding Marvel DVDs all day. Roll on this year's James Bond film.'

'Thought you only liked the Sean Connery ones,' I said, laughing.

He pulled a face. 'That's not the point. When I hear that theme tune, I'll know that the madness is almost over, and I can start to wind down and look forward to the return of normality. Boxing Day's the best day in my opinion. No pressure to have a good time or follow a timetable. But at least once the kids are in bed on Christmas night and us grown-ups are settled in front of the telly, we're on the home stretch. A few beers, a mince pie and bed. Bliss.' He closed his eyes for a moment, a wide smile on his face as he clearly pictured the scene. Penny nudged him and he winked at me. 'Have a good one, Katy.'

They drove off and I waved until they turned the corner, then headed to the staff car park at the back of the shop. Whatever Mike said I knew perfectly well that they'd have a fabulous Christmas. They'd been looking forward to it for weeks and it would, no doubt, run like clockwork. Even if it didn't, that would only add to their fun. Christmas was made for families like the Miltons if you ask me.

My little Fiat stood tiny and forlorn next to Kerry's family-sized BMW. I frowned, suddenly realising that Matt's car was missing. My heart thudded. Had it been stolen? I looked around frantically, as if I'd find clues in the snow, but there were no footprints, no tyre tracks…

Then it dawned on me. Matt and Kerry must have arrived together that morning, and no doubt they'd be leaving together too. He was going home with her, wasn't he?

I was happy for them, obviously. I'm not such a mean-spirited person that I begrudge anyone a bit of romance. Even so, I couldn't help feeling a pang of loss. Was I the only person in the world spending Christmas all alone?

Breaking up with someone is always painful, I guess, but when you must work at the very place where it all began, it's a constant reminder. Unfortunately for me, Special Occasions is where Simon first wandered into my life.

***

I can't say it was love at first sight when I met him. In fact, in the interests of absolute honesty, I should declare here and now that I'd thought he was a bit of a prat when he strolled into the shop a week or so before Christmas, a whole seven years ago, looking for an "extra-special card for a very special lady". Naturally, I'd assumed he meant a wife or girlfriend, and steered him to the appropriate section, only to have him laugh and tell me he wanted a card for his boss.

Apparently, they were having a whip-round at work to get this super-talented, exceptionally wonderful human being something lovely for Christmas, and Simon had volunteered to buy the card and organise the present for her.

'You won't know her by face, but you've probably seen her name on the credits.'

'Credits?'

He gave me a smug smile. '*East Riding Round-Up*. Don't pretend you didn't recognise me. I'm in your home every evening, after all.'

I shrugged, embarrassed to admit I never watched *East Riding Round-Up*. We were usually in the kitchen having tea between six and six-thirty when it was on, and if we did ever make it into the living room at that time, we mostly watched *Look North* or *Calendar*.

'Simon,' he said, giving me a megawatt smile. 'Simon Henley. Your friendly local reporter.'

'O-kay,' I dragged out, thinking, *what a numpty*.

Looking back, as I watched him choose the most simpering, grovelling card imaginable, I recall that I felt zero attraction or even any respect for him. He left the shop and I forgot all about him.

Two days later he was back, looking for another Christmas card for a special lady.

'Another one?' I said, raising an eyebrow. 'Who is it this time?'

'A rather attractive and wonderful woman who has quite won my heart,' he confessed. 'I really need to make a big impression on her. Do you think you could help me?'

He seemed different; there was a vulnerability and an awkwardness that I hadn't seen on his previous visit. As we searched through the racks of soppy cards, bearing cute little drawings of teddy bear couples embracing under mistletoe, or artistic images of romantic sleigh rides for two, or cartoons of loved-up reindeer, I answered him as honestly as I could when he questioned me as to the suitability of each card.

'Too sentimental,' I told him, as he held up a card bearing a verse that was nauseatingly slushy. 'Too jokey,' I added, as he pointed to a drawing of Mrs Claus rolling her eyes in dismay as Santa snored drunkenly in a chair. 'Too rude,' I muttered, hastily hiding a card that carried an extremely risqué joke about a snowman and his carrot.

Eventually, we settled on the perfect card and headed over to the counter, where I scanned the barcode and waited for payment.

'Do you have a pen I can borrow?' he asked, handing me a couple of pound coins. 'Sorry, I don't know your name.'

'It's Katy, and sure.' I handed him the pen and began to tidy the space behind the counter which, after a day of frantic activity had become rather disorganised.

'There you go, Katy. Your pen.'

I nodded. 'Thanks. Merry Christmas.'

'Merry Christmas. Oh, and this is for you.'

I'd blushed to my hair roots as he handed me the card. 'For me?' Was he joking?

'Absolutely. And if you don't like it, it's your fault, because you chose it.'

'But I thought — I thought you said it was for a special lady?'

'I can't imagine anyone more special. I haven't been able to stop thinking about you. Ever since I came in here the other day, you've been on my mind.'

He leaned on the counter, smiling, and feeling suddenly a bit weak-kneed and trembly, I smiled back, noticing for the first time how blue his eyes were, and what a well-shaped and thoroughly kissable mouth he had.

'So, Katy, I expect you have plans for Christmas Day?'

'Er, yes. I do.'

'So how about Boxing Day?'

'Boxing Day?' I'd stared at him stupidly, not grasping what he meant.

'I'd like to take you out on a date,' he'd said gently. 'That's if you'd like me to, of course.'

It struck me how incredibly sophisticated he was, and I felt my stomach give a little flutter. Of course, I only had a couple of previous boyfriends to compare him to, and since they were around my age and neither of them had even possessed a suit, a smartly dressed, well-groomed man like Simon was bound to seem different. Impressive even. Gazing into those blue eyes of his at that moment, I'd suddenly felt there was nothing I'd like more than to go out with him. I thought it was the most romantic thing anyone had ever done, and Mum agreed when I told her about it over tea that night.

Dad, on the other hand, mimed sticking two fingers down his throat and informed us that it was the cheesiest thing he'd ever heard of, and that "that bloke sounds like a total creep", but we ignored him. What did dads know about such matters, after all?

As I got to know Simon better, I found myself agreeing with Dad's opinions on my boyfriend far too often for my liking, but I became a master at ignoring my own doubts. Just shows you. Always trust your instincts — and your dad.

Chapter 2
Step Into Christmas

I cleared the snow from the windscreen of my little Fiat and set off. I had to call at the supermarket before I headed out of Hull. I needed something for Christmas dinner and some general provisions. There'd be nothing at the caravan. I should really have made a list, I thought, hoping that by now the shopping frenzy would have died down.

No such luck. After driving round and round for a full ten minutes, muttering and cursing as I was outmanoeuvred by aggressive dads with reindeer antlers on their heads, and harassed mothers in tears, I managed to squeeze myself into a space at the far end of the car park and crunched through the snow to the main entrance of the supermarket.

I had to push my way into the store and sighed as I saw what looked like the entire population of East Yorkshire dashing round the aisles with fully laden trolleys and manic expressions on their faces. Here we go then, I thought, picking up a basket.

It was much harder than I'd expected, Christmas shopping for one when the aisles were heaving with happy families and loved-up couples. I kept noticing last-minute bargains and special offers and caught myself thinking, *Simon would like those*, before realising that it was none of my business any longer what Simon liked. At least I wouldn't have to buy dates this year. Even Dad had laughed when I told him how much Simon loved them and that we always had to have a box in for Christmas.

'How old's this bloke again? Sixty-six? Told you he was too old for you.'

'He's only seven years older than me, Dad.'

'In some ways he's seventy years older,' he'd said, giving me a knowing look, 'but in others he's a big, daft kid. You should think on.'

I mean, what was I supposed to make of that? And how could I take him seriously anyway? This was, after all, coming from a man of sixty-one who could eat a whole packet of dates to himself, and did so every Christmas. I'd only told him in the hope it would make him like Simon a bit more; make him realise that they did have things in common after all, even if it was only a festive tradition of stuffing their faces with dried fruit. I'd always tried to think of ways of convincing my dad that Simon wasn't so bad, because I'd known he wasn't keen on my boyfriend from the very start.

***

I'd only been going out with him officially for a few days and, to me, we weren't even in a proper relationship, yet Simon had been surprisingly keen to meet my parents and, *un*surprisingly, my mum had begged to meet him. She couldn't get over the fact that I was dating a "television star" as she termed him, with gross exaggeration. She told all her friends about him and conveniently forgot to mention that, until I'd started seeing him, she'd never so much as glanced at

East Riding Round-Up. She insisted I invite him round for tea on New Year's Eve.

'I've got a party to go to,' I told her.

'Oh, a party! Lots of drunk people and noise and mess, and then all that palaver getting home afterwards, and double fare for a taxi. Better off staying in for once.' She narrowed her eyes. 'Don't you want us to meet him? Are we not good enough for a television star? Are you ashamed of us?'

After that, I felt I had no choice but to invite him and, to my astonishment, he accepted. I'd assumed he'd already have plans and Dad thought it was highly suspicious that he didn't.

'Hasn't this bloke got any mates?' he'd grumbled, clearly put out that his favourite night of the year was going to be disrupted by my boyfriend. Dad liked nothing better than to slouch in front of the television, sipping beer and stuffing his face with chocolate on New Year's Eve. Mum made him watch his weight and monitored his drinking all year, and between Christmas Eve and New Year's Eve was the only time he could do what he liked, so he hated having guests to spoil it all.

Despite Mum's fussing and the fact that our house had been polished, dusted and vacuumed to hotel standards and a buffet prepared that would have been acceptable at a society wedding, we couldn't cheer him up, and he refused to get changed, insisting there was plenty of time and that we should stop mithering him.

Mum and I were mortified when Simon arrived a little early, to discover Dad still sitting in his pyjamas, a paper crown from a Christmas cracker on his head, and his hand firmly wedged in the tin of Roses.

Mum had nearly died of shame and had miraculously managed to swipe both the hat and the chocolates in one deft movement as she urged Simon to sit, told him how much they'd been looking forward to meeting him, and offered him a choice of drinks all in one breath.

I'd sat there, glowing with pride, as he told them all about his job, his family, his upbringing, his friends, and his hobbies.

Mum had hung on his every word, oohing and aahing as he filled her in with behind-the-scenes gossip from the studios, even though she had no idea who on earth he was talking about. She'd even offered him a glass of her precious Baileys Irish Cream and managed not to wince too much when he accepted.

Dad had seemed less impressed — not least that a bloke would drink such a "girly" beverage — and I'd fidgeted a little uncomfortably as I noticed him rolling his eyes a couple of times as he defied Mum's glares and sucked ferociously on the strawberry creams, still wearing his tartan pyjamas.

When Simon had finally left for home, Mum had gushed what a charming and handsome man he was.

Dad fixed me with a weary look and said, 'By heck, Katy, he's a right boring bugger isn't he?'

I'd been furious and had defended Simon fiercely, with Mum's backing.

Dad had held up his hands in defeat. 'All right, all right, keep your hair on. I was only saying.'

'Well don't,' Mum snapped. 'Keep your opinions to yourself. And—' she'd added, whipping the tin of Roses from his grasp, 'that's quite enough chocolate for you for one day, thank you very much.'

***

The checkout girl looked a bit stunned as, forty-five minutes later, I dumped my meagre amount of shopping on the conveyer belt and wiped the sweat from my fevered brow.

'These are on offer: buy two get one free,' she informed me, waving the box of Quality Street at me, and giving me a kindly smile.

'Thanks, but I only need one,' I said.

She seemed to take my refusal as a personal insult and glared at me as if I'd done something unspeakable. She scanned the chocolates with a scowl on her face, not even bothering to ask if I needed any help with my packing, which was a first. Not that I needed help, given the tiny amount of shopping I'd done.

Behind me a queue of exhausted parents had built up. They leaned on their trolleys, which were packed full to the brim with festive goodies and muttered to each other about how ridiculous it all was for just one day.

Above the relentless din of whining children and couples arguing about how much beer they'd really need and whether sprouts were truly essential, Band Aid were asking Do They Know It's Christmas?

I thought, with a distinct lack of seasonal spirit, that I wished I was somewhere right now where no one had a clue.

The checkout girl gave me a knowing look as she scanned the toilet roll, soap, coffee, milk, bread, and microwave turkey dinner for one. I saw pity in her eyes as I stuffed the shopping into two carrier bags and took out my credit card. Briefly I wished I was still wearing my engagement ring, just to show her I wasn't some sad, lonely loser.

Unfortunately, I'd posted it back to Simon, determined to show him that I was getting on with my life and not in the slightest bit bothered about being heartlessly cast aside, so maybe I *was* some sad, lonely loser after all.

For the first time I regretted sending it back. God knows, it had taken me long enough to get the damn ring in the first place.

'I said, is there anything else I can help you with?' The checkout lady's voice disturbed my train of thought, which was probably a good thing.

Blinking away the memories I mumbled, 'Sorry? Oh no, nothing thanks.'

She shook her head slightly and handed me the receipt. 'There you go, love. Merry Christmas.'

'Thanks. You too.'

Judging by the sympathetic smile she gave me she'd evidently forgiven my earlier ungracious behaviour and had decided I was one of the poor unfortunate souls that she should be extra kind to at this special time of year.

Though, from where I was standing, it didn't feel very special. Not this year. I had an overwhelming feeling it wasn't going to be much of a merry Christmas. Maybe I should have taken the checkout lady up on her offer of three boxes of Quality Street for the price of two after all.

Chapter 3
Driving Home for Christmas

I'd been in the supermarket for nearly an hour, thanks to all the crazed shoppers who were practically having fist fights over the last packet of Paxo. I needed to get a move on. It was gone five already.

Normally the drive from Hull to Weltringham took around thirty minutes, but with people heading home for the holidays and the unexpected snow, it was well over an hour before I even got close to the coast. If I'd been going to my parents' house I'd have been home ages ago, I thought, feeling very sorry for myself as I drove through little villages, seeing fairy lights twinkling in the windows of houses as I passed and thinking enviously of families in their living rooms, all cosy and snug and loved.

I felt terribly alone and unwanted, and rather like *The Little Match Girl*.

I mean, what were Mum and Dad playing at anyway, going away for Christmas? Who does that? Christmas means home and family, right?

They'd booked the cruise just days before I was going to ask them about spending Christmas at their place, and in my less emotional and more unselfish moments I knew it served me right for making assumptions. It was the first time they'd ever gone away for the festive season, and I suppose I'd just taken for granted that they would be there for me.

They were really excited about their first ever cruise, and I didn't want them to feel guilty about abandoning me, so I never told them I was being brutally ejected onto the streets. They thought I was spending Christmas with Penny and Mike, and I — rather nobly, I thought — had made the decision to let them go on thinking that.

I had a key to their house and, if push came to shove, I could have gone there, but Mrs Ketley next door was like a private investigator, the way she nosed into everyone's business. I had no doubt she'd be keeping an eye on the place while Mum and Dad were away, so there'd be no chance that I could stay there without her noticing, which would mean my parents would find out as soon as they got home. They'd be devastated if they learned that I'd spent Christmas all alone. It was best all round if I stayed away.

They'd never have gone if they hadn't thought I was going to have a good time at Penny's, especially not after what had happened with Simon. Even Mum had totally changed her opinion of him, and goodness knows, she'd once been his biggest fan. She'd been terribly impatient in the early days of our relationship, constantly asking me if there was any sign of wedding bells and urging me to give Simon a nudge. I'd had to tell her, as gently as I could, to back off and allow things to develop at their own pace.

Of course, when it all went wrong she'd been mortified, blaming herself for pushing me into an engagement with a man who was clearly not worthy of me. I told her the truth; she hadn't pushed me. I'd jumped. Far too willingly.

***

We'd been going out for four whole years before Simon finally popped the question.

As Christmas approached, I'd had a feeling that he was going to ask me to marry him. It wasn't anything specific, but there'd been vague mentions of marriage and settling down during the previous months, and grim allusions to his age. I think he'd just found his first grey hair and at the ripe old age of thirty-four he was beginning to feel a bit past it. Can't have been easy having a glamorous younger woman as a girlfriend, obviously. Ha!

Thinking back, it's hard to imagine that I was beside myself with excitement at the prospect, but I can't deny it's true.

I loved Simon. I loved the way he'd happily cook the tea if he got home before me; how, after a long day on my feet, he'd run me a hot bath and light candles for me; I loved how self-assured and confident he was, because that made me feel safe, even when we were at local media events that would normally have terrified me; I loved how intelligent he was, how cultured. Compared to me he was a genius. I knew little about art or music or local heritage. Simon seemed to be the font of all knowledge and was happy to fill in some of the many gaps in my education. He was smart and handsome, and I felt very lucky to have him as a boyfriend. Having him as a husband seemed like the stuff of dreams.

But as the years rolled on, I'd begun to believe it was never going to happen and had been getting rather fed up, wondering if there was any point to a relationship that didn't seem to be moving on. I'd confided my worries to Mum, and she'd been quick to reassure me that Simon loved me, and that it would happen eventually, I just had to be patient, which was quite a turnaround given I'd spent ages telling her the same thing.

When December arrived, I had a strong feeling that she was right and began to imagine a romantic Christmas Day proposal. I wondered what sort of ring he'd chosen and hoped I'd like it. Did he even know my size? Maybe I'd have to take it back to be altered. Then again, what did that matter? Would we have an engagement party? How would he pop the question?

I daydreamed endlessly, imagining him down on one knee in front of the Christmas tree, while Mum and Dad thoughtfully made themselves scarce — Dad having previously been asked for permission to marry me by Simon, as tradition demanded.

Or would he take me out for a candlelit dinner somewhere? I hoped he'd remembered to book somewhere if that was his plan. It was difficult to get a table in a decent restaurant so close to Christmas.

As it turned out, I needn't have worried. Christmas came and went without so much as a mention of marriage, which cut me to the quick. I did a sterling job of smiling when I unwrapped the DVD boxset of one of my favourite programmes, and a bottle of expensive perfume on Christmas morning. Maybe he'd propose when I saw him that evening? Mum had invited him to have tea with us and I was sure he must be planning to ask me to marry him then.

Nope. After battling severe disappointment, I told myself it didn't matter, and I didn't even care about getting married. Maybe Simon wasn't the one for me after all? Our relationship was clearly going nowhere. Then the day after Boxing Day, not a special day at all, Simon casually mentioned that he'd been thinking that maybe it was time we "got hitched".

It seemed that his colleagues and friends were hinting that it was time we were married, and, in hindsight, it would probably be good for his career.

'If we pool our savings, we should be able to afford somewhere decent to live, too,' he'd added thoughtfully. 'The more I think about it, the more it makes sense. What do you reckon?'

It was hardly moonlight and roses was it? Underwhelmed doesn't begin to cover how I felt.

I'd been stupid enough to overlook all that. I'd pushed all my disappointment and doubts aside and had delightedly shared with my parents that I was finally engaged to the man of my dreams. Mum, naturally, was ecstatic. Dad, though, hadn't been exactly thrilled.

'You sure about this, love?' he'd asked, his forehead creased with doubt. 'It's a big step, after all.'

'Of course she's sure. Honestly, what a thing to say,' Mum muttered, giving him a warning look. 'Don't start all that again, anyway. Today's a happy day.'

He'd frowned, waving his hand at her dismissively. 'Don't tell me what I can and can't say to my own daughter. I'm just asking her to think about it, that's all. Divorces are bloody expensive, you know.'

'Oh, Dad!' I'd half laughed, but I was quite hurt deep down, even though I wasn't really surprised. I knew Dad wasn't keen on Simon and probably never would be.

Mum tutted. 'I don't know what's wrong with you, honestly I don't. Fancy being so negative on the very day your daughter gets engaged. Well, I'm going to open a bottle of wine to celebrate.'

She hurried into the kitchen and Dad looked at me, his expression serious. 'I wouldn't normally tell you this, love,' he'd murmured, 'but this is a big decision and I think you should know all the facts.'

My stomach had lurched with anxiety. 'What are you on about, Dad?'

'Your mum's been interfering again. She tipped Simon off that you were thinking about finishing with him 'cos he hadn't popped the question. Warned him that if he didn't get a move on, you'd look for someone who was more likely to commit.'

I felt sick. 'She did what?'

'Aye, I know. You don't have to tell me,' he said with a sigh. 'I told her she was wrong and should stay out of it, but you know your mother. Always thinks she knows what's best. Don't be too hard on her, love. She was only thinking of you, but, well I reckon you might want to think again now, right?'

I'd tried to push his words away and pretend that everything was fine, but I couldn't manage it. Eventually, when Mum had downed a couple of glasses of wine and was more likely to tell me the truth, I asked her why she'd said such a thing to Simon.

'Your bloody father!' She glared at him. 'What did you want to go and tell her that for? Now it's all spoilt for her.'

'So, Simon didn't want to marry me at all?' I felt nauseated. I'd been made a complete fool of.

Mum shrieked at me and waved her glass in my direction, spilling wine all over her precious carpet. 'Don't be daft! Course he wanted to marry you. I just gave him a nudge, that's all. I didn't want you to do anything stupid like finishing with him, when I could tell he thinks the world of you. I just pointed out that four years is a long time to be together without any sort of commitment and that, as a woman, you had to remember your body clock and—'

'Oh, Mum,' I groaned, mortified.

'Don't *Oh, Mum*, me,' she snapped. 'I'm telling you he was grateful I'd mentioned it. He said he'd been thinking about asking you for ages but just hadn't plucked up the courage in case you turned him down.'

'Bloody wimp,' Dad muttered.

'He's not a wimp,' she protested. 'He's a thoughtful young man and he's going places, I'm telling you. He's got ambition, Katy. You could have a great life with him. You should be thrilled that such a decent fella is keen to marry you and make a life with you. And he is, really he is. Stop mithering and enjoy being engaged, for God's sake. We've got a wedding to plan.'

Draining my glass of wine, I'd decided she was right, and I was being stupid. Simon loved me. Why else would he want to get married? Maybe Mum had given him a slight nudge, but she hadn't forced him into doing anything he hadn't already wanted to do.

Simon hadn't wanted to choose a ring for me, saying it was far too important to risk making a mistake, and that he'd much rather I went with him. We ended up browsing the jewellery stores in town a week later and got a real bargain because of the New Year sales.

After some persuasion, I'd agreed to put the wedding off for a year, so that we could buy our first home together. Simon said that had to be the priority, and he was quite correct of course. After all, a wedding is all very well and good, but you must have somewhere to live, right? We could hardly bunk in with Mum and

Dad, and I knew, having met Simon's parents twice, that hell would freeze over before they asked me to move in there.

We pooled our savings, as he'd suggested, and got a mortgage on a lovely one-bedroomed flat in town. Dad wasn't too sure about that either.

'Wouldn't you be better off with a nice little house? These swanky flats are all well and good, but you can't add value can you? And there's no room to swing a cat in here.'

'How can you say that?' Mum had demanded. 'Look at the beautiful kitchen! Granite worktops, Dave! Granite!' She'd run her fingers along the worktop lovingly. 'And have you seen the posh radiator in the bathroom? Ooh, we could have one like that in our bathroom, couldn't we?'

Dad tutted, clearly unimpressed. 'All fur coat and no knickers if you ask me,' he muttered. 'Give me a nice, solid, terraced house any day of the week.'

Ironically, until that moment, I'd been thinking the same thing. A flat was no place for the dog I was desperate to own, and despite Simon's assurances, I was sure that buying a house on the outskirts of the city would make our money go further. Dad's negativity, however, spurred me to my fiancé's defence. Defiantly, I assured him that city centre property nearly always held its value and that being so close to work for both of us was a huge bonus, as it meant we would save on travel expenses, and would be far more convenient — especially for Simon, who often got called in at short notice. He couldn't argue with that, or maybe he could but had waved the white flag.

Anyway, Simon and I put down the deposit and moved in together. With it being a reasonably new property there wasn't much that needed doing to the place, so we could, I thought, start saving for the wedding and begin making plans.

Dad had already agreed to chip in to help pay for the wedding, but I could see that he still wasn't happy about my forthcoming marriage.

Luckily for him, Simon was in no hurry.

The months went by without a single plan being made, or any real discussion about the wedding. By April, I was beginning to wonder if I'd dreamt the whole thing, and only the ring on my finger proved the engagement had really happened.

With a bit of coaxing from Mum, I took matters into my own hands and suggested a date in September, but Simon wasn't having it. It turned out that, against all my expectations, he wanted a big church wedding with all the trimmings; the sort of wedding that simply couldn't and shouldn't be rushed. Simon insisted that it would take a lot of organising and maybe we should start planning it later.

'Let's get this year over with first,' he'd said, despite it only being spring. 'We'll start making plans on the other side of Christmas.'

I'd learned very early in our relationship that *the other side of Christmas* was his favourite time of year. He was always going to do things then. The twenty-fifth of December seemed to be the major landmark in his life — not for the usual reasons, but because everything important was scheduled to take place once it was out of the way. I'd thought it was quite sensible of him at first, but there you go. You live and learn.

Chapter 4
Let it Snow, Let it Snow, Let it Snow

I turned on the radio, desperate for some cheer as I drove along the dark, winding country lanes. As the music blared out, I groaned.

'Oh no, not again!'

Honestly, if I heard Do They Know It's Christmas? once more I would wrench the radio out with my bare hands.

Why did we have to move so far away? And why did a bit of snow make such a short journey so much lengthier and more difficult? Why did I ever listen to Simon in the first place? Why did it have to be my shop he walked into that day?

Too many questions and not enough answers. I rubbed my forehead and tried to concentrate on the road, relieved as the song faded away, then sighing when Slade's Merry Christmas Everybody took its place. Same old music, year in, year out. I wondered why I had never noticed how repetitive it all was way before. Why had it never driven me mad?

Maybe because I'd never nursed a broken heart until now — and it wasn't for Simon.

Someone careered around the bend in the road, headlights on full, dazzling me.

'Idiot!' I screeched, alarmed.

Concentrate, Katy. There's no hurry to reach home.

Home. It hardly seemed like that anymore. Had it ever, really? We'd bought it when we were full of hope, and it had all seemed like an amazing adventure.

***

Penny thought I was mad when I told her about our plans to move on from our city centre flat and, typically, made no attempt to hide her horror.

'Why would you want to live all the way out there? It's the back of beyond. There isn't even a Tesco. It will take you ages to get into work every morning and what if something goes wrong with your car?'

'We have two cars,' I'd reminded her, 'and if anything goes wrong with mine, I'm sure Simon can give me a lift in his. He only works a ten-minute drive away from the shop, for goodness' sake. And who cares about a Tesco? There's a cute little post office and general store. We can do our big shop on the way home after work anyway.'

Blimey, talk about blind faith.

'But it's so dreary,' she'd protested. 'Even the roads commit suicide round there.'

That was hardly fair, although it *was* true that the Holderness coast was eroding fast and many roads had crumbled away into the sea, but the village of Weltringham was a fair way from the cliff edge and Cartwheel Cottage was in no danger. Well, not in my lifetime anyway.

It had taken a while for Simon to convince me that living there was what I wanted, but I'd totally come around to his way of thinking.

Weltringham was surrounded on three sides by fields and farmland and when we'd first visited the village — to look at a car Simon was considering buying, though he eventually decided against it — it was early summer; the fields were a blaze of bright yellow oilseed rape, and the verges were draped in frothy cow parsley.

It was like a little piece of heaven on earth, so different from the concrete streets we lived and worked in. I couldn't imagine anyone going there and *not* falling in love with it, though, come to think of it, living there had been all Simon's idea.

We'd started making wedding plans and had got as far as booking the church when he came home one evening in May and said he'd been thinking about our living arrangements. Apparently, simply everyone in his office lived in the country and commuted into the city for work and he felt we should too.

'Who's everyone?' I'd demanded suspiciously.

He'd gone all vague and blustery and I'd just known what he was going to say. Eventually he admitted that by *everyone*, he meant Kevin Dowd, another reporter who he considered to be his nemesis, since Kevin kept getting — in Simon's opinion — all the best jobs, despite being a *whole three years* younger than him.

Whatever Kevin had, Simon always wanted something at least as good — and mostly better — than him.

Not long after our engagement, I discovered that Kevin had got engaged just a week before us. Of course, he'd been all romantic and taken his girlfriend out for a special Christmas Eve meal, presenting her with a gorgeous diamond solitaire while their fellow diners looked on. Simon must have found out on the very day he asked me to marry him. Another reason I had my doubts that he'd really meant his proposal but, yet again, I ignored that nagging voice in my head.

Now it seemed, Wonderboy, as Simon had dubbed him, had bought a nice little place in the sticks and had been boasting about it ever since, something that Simon simply couldn't tolerate.

'But what's wrong with this place?' I'd demanded, looking round our little flat in bewilderment. Admittedly, I'd had my doubts about the place before we took the plunge and bought it, but we'd been happy here. It was very handy for all the shops, cinemas, and bars, after all. Even better, we weren't far from the marina and liked to stroll round there on warm evenings, gazing enviously at the yachts and sipping drinks as we soaked up the sun and planned our future.

'It's fine for a young couple,' said Simon, as if we were in our dotage, 'but once we're married things will be different. Besides, I'm too close to work. I want to put a bit of distance between my home and the studios. I can't switch off. I don't think you realise how stressful it is, being on television. I can't leave the building without someone recognising me.'

That was a big fat fib, and I knew it. I'd been at Simon's side as we wandered around the city centre, and it seemed to me that very few people ever gave him so much as a second glance. Even the ones who did seem to recognise him would merely look at him with a puzzled expression, as if wondering where they knew him from. I thought he had rather an over-inflated opinion of himself, but I said nothing. After all, he was right. I didn't know how it felt to be on television. Maybe Simon had a point.

'We should sell this place and buy somewhere in one of the villages. There are some real bargains to be had if you look in the right place,' he continued. 'I've been searching online, and it's been a real eye-opener, I can tell you.'

'I'm not sure—'

'You could have that dog you keep going on about,' he said quickly. 'Something neat and tidy that doesn't shed.'

'Really?'

'Yes. I mean, so long as it doesn't bark much. I can't be doing with a dog that yaps. And not a puppy because of the chewing and the housetraining. And not one that needs a lot of exercise or stimulation. But some sort of older dog that's been well-trained. I'm sure we can find one at a breeder's somewhere.'

So, a dog that didn't shed, didn't chew, didn't bark, and didn't need exercising or housetraining. Never mind a breeder, I had a feeling we'd be better off looking for Simon's perfect dog in a toy shop. Still, I was sure that, once I found the dog I loved, Simon would love it too. All in good time. At least if we lived in an actual house, I could start looking at last.

'But can we afford to move, what with the wedding and everything?'

I was doubtful. Simon's plans for the reception alone would stretch our finances. Mum and Dad were happy to help but I couldn't expect them to pay for it all. Not with the extravagant event Simon envisioned.

'I think the house is more important than the wedding,' he said firmly.

'Fine,' I agreed. 'So, we scale back the reception? I'm happy with that. And we can halve the number of guests we invite. I don't know who most of the people on this list are, anyway.'

'What are you talking about?' Simon looked at me, aghast. 'This is a once-in-a-lifetime event. My parents would be mortified if we scaled it down. This is important to them.'

I couldn't help thinking that, if it was so important, why didn't they offer to chip in and help pay for it then? We hadn't had so much as an engagement card from them so, frankly, I didn't give a monkey's what sort of wedding they wanted.

'I think we should put the wedding off for a while,' Simon mused. 'We need to get the house sorted first. It's a question of priorities. We'll spend this year finding our new home and we'll start planning the wedding again on the other side of Christmas.'

Oh, that dreaded phrase again! I'd taken some persuading, but Simon convinced me somehow that we were doing the right thing. After all, what was another year when we had the rest of our lives together?

Having made up our minds, Weltringham was the obvious place to start looking, given how much we'd loved it when we'd visited the previous summer. Penny wasn't the only one who thought we were mad, but we were determined to live our dream.

It wasn't easy to find somewhere for sale around there and the months dragged on. We scoured online property sites, trekked around estate agents' offices, and asked all our friends and family to keep a look out for any suitable properties.

Then Cartwheel Cottage came up for auction.

We took Penny and Mike to view it with us and they were visibly appalled.

Mike's mouth dropped open as he stared at the object of our desire in disbelief. 'You two lost the plot or something?' he said at last. 'Have you any idea how much work it would take to even make this habitable?'

'It's a wreck,' wailed Penny. 'Please don't even think about buying it. You do know Yorkie Homes are building a new estate not twenty minutes from us? Why don't you check out their brochure?'

Simon and I looked at each other, smug in the knowledge that we could see something they couldn't. Don't ask me what it was. Thinking about it now and remembering the state it was in, I can't imagine why we fell in love with the place. You know when you go somewhere, and you just get that *feeling*? Like, even though you've never been there before, somehow it's already home? It was like that.

Looking around, I could already visualise our children running around the garden, hear their laughter and chatter echoing round the empty rooms.

I didn't see cobweb-strewn beams and grimy glass and peeling paint: I saw a cosy fire flickering in the grate, and a Christmas tree in the corner of the room; a couple of toddlers splashing in a paddling pool on the newly-mown lawn, and a scruffy-looking dog racing around in excitement as they flicked water at him; I saw a chunky oak sideboard, where framed photographs of Simon and me on our wedding day, and our children, all fair hair and blue eyes like their daddy, took pride of place. I didn't smell mould and damp; I smelt baby powder and cinnamon and woodsmoke and a turkey roasting in an oven and summer flowers and freshly cut grass.

Cartwheel Cottage, a run-down shell of a building in urgent need of restoration, had totally won my heart and, looking at Simon's shining eyes, I knew he felt the same.

'I bet that's where Lord Lucan's been hiding out,' said Penny, nodding towards the weeds which stood shoulder high in some parts of a garden which stretched for a quarter of an acre. 'You're mad, the pair of you.'

Maybe we had been. We'd certainly been unrealistic and overly optimistic. Despite all the warnings from our friends — repeated with force by my parents when they came with us to view it a second time — we were determined to secure our dream home.

Life became a whirlwind of visits to the bank, showing prospective buyers around our flat, working through our finances, and dealing with an agony of mixed emotions. We veered chaotically between the pleasure and excitement of imagining living out our rural dream, and utter despair when we convinced ourselves that we would lose the cottage.

But, against all odds, ours had been the winning bid. By September Cartwheel Cottage belonged to us.

***

Looking back, we were incredibly naïve.

We'd thought that, once the cottage was ours, it would be plain sailing. We hadn't realised how long it would take to find an architect, draw up plans, get planning permission.

Oh, planning permission — the two most hated words in the dictionary. The battle for Cartwheel Cottage seemed to drag on longer than the Wars of the Roses. Another autumn came and went, and it was obvious that the wedding would have to remain on hold. Our new home drained all our spare time and our finances.

'Never mind,' soothed Simon. 'We'll spend the next year getting the cottage just perfect and then we'll book the wedding on the other side of Christmas.'

Mum was a bit upset about yet another delay.

'I've already bought my hat,' she moaned.

Dad tutted. 'They don't have a bloody sell-by date on them, Moira. It won't go off, you know.'

'Men! What do you know about it?' she demanded. 'This time next year it might be out of fashion. I may have decided on a different colour entirely. I might have seen one I like better. Oh well, never mind. It's only money.'

'Aye, my bloody money,' Dad said with a sigh. 'But what's a week's wages, as long as it makes you happy?'

Mum ignored the jibe. 'Do you think you're ever going to get as far as booking an actual venue?' she asked wistfully. 'Only, people are beginning to ask questions you know.'

'What sort of questions?' I said, feeling irritable. What business was it of anyone else's anyway? 'And what people?'

'Nosy sods,' Dad said. 'Probably your Auntie Jane and Magnum PI next door.'

'Don't be so mean,' Mum said. 'They're just concerned, that's all. They know how desperate Katy is to get married.'

'I'm not desperate!' I gasped, horrified. Is that what people thought? 'There's no hurry at all.'

'Well, you are getting on a bit,' she pointed out. 'Time's ticking on you know.'

'Oh, aye,' Dad said, giving me a knowing wink. 'Hats might not go off, but your eggs will.'

'Do you mind?' I spluttered. 'I'm only in my twenties!'

'You don't have to tell me,' he assured me. 'It's your mother that's fretting about your eggs, not me. I couldn't give a monkey's, but she thinks they'll be hard boiled or summat.'

'Well, for your information, we haven't even discussed having children yet.'

And we probably won't until Wonderboy, Kevin bloody Dowd, fathers one.

'The most important thing right now is getting Cartwheel Cottage into order,' I said, pushing such treacherous thoughts aside. 'No point worrying about the wedding or kids until we have a decent home is there?'

'Hmm. I suppose not,' Mum acknowledged, somewhat reluctantly.

'And I reckon it's going to take a good while to get it into shape,' Dad said, sounding suspiciously cheerful about it. 'Are you sure you can't take that hat back to the shop, Moira?'

***

Mike helped us find a reputable builder. 'He did a brilliant extension on my cousin's house. Doesn't live far from your place. Here's his number,' he said, handing me a business card for a company called LI Builders.

LI himself turned out to be Luke Ingledew, a quiet, dark-haired man in his early thirties. He'd sold his house and had moved back in with his parents who ran The Seagull Inn, just a fifteen-minute walk from the cottage, while he looked around for another renovation project.

I liked him immediately, particularly when he turned up with a scruffy looking dog, about the size of a Westie, but with smoky grey, wiry hair that half covered his big brown eyes.

'Oh, isn't he lovely!' I was delighted when the dog ran up to me and wagged his tail, clearly eager to make friends.

Luke grinned. 'That's Pip,' he told me. 'He's a real character. I wouldn't be without him.'

'But you don't bring him to work?' Simon looked appalled at the idea.

'Oh, but it wouldn't matter if he did would it?' I said, not wanting him to upset Luke before he'd even started work. Besides, what harm could it do? And this little fella was so adorable. I couldn't help but notice that he bore a startling resemblance to the dog of my imagination — the scruffy little mutt that played joyfully in the garden with my future children. 'What sort of dog is he?' I enquired, thinking I could maybe get a similar dog one day.

Luke shook his head. 'Anyone's guess,' he admitted. 'I got him from a rescue centre when he was a year old. He's four now. He was found wandering the streets a few weeks before I met him, so no one knew what breed either of his parents was. Best guess is there's some terrier in him somewhere, but other than that… And no,' he added, his voice suddenly becoming more formal as he turned to Simon, 'I won't be bringing him with me to work. A building site's not safe for a dog and I wouldn't want him to get hurt, would I?'

'Well, quite.' Simon squirmed as Luke gave him a pleasant smile. It was quite clear who'd come out top in that little discussion.

Luke examined our plans, negotiated terms and prices with Simon, and started work in late February.

He certainly seemed to know what he was doing, and I quickly grew to trust his judgment. Unfortunately, I couldn't say the same about Simon. For some bewildering reason, my fiancé had decided we didn't need a project manager as he was more than capable of organising everything himself, even though he had no experience whatsoever of renovating a property.

He didn't particularly like Luke, and I got the feeling it was mutual. There were lots of disagreements and a great deal of tension as they stamped around the cottage, and I knew Simon would have happily sacked him if he'd thought he could get anyone else for the same price. Things would have been done a lot quicker if they'd co-operated, but everything became a battle. You could practically smell the testosterone as they locked horns and fought for supremacy.

'He's arrogant, that's the trouble,' Simon raged one evening, as we unwrapped our Chinese takeaway in the tiny kitchen of the house we'd temporarily rented on the outskirts of Hull. 'He thinks he knows best about everything.'

'Well, he is a builder,' I began tentatively, my mouth watering as I spooned chicken fried rice onto my plate. I was starving, not having eaten since early that morning.

Simon was having none of it. 'I think he forgets that it's our home. What we say should go and no questions asked.'

I said nothing, not wanting to get into an argument about it. I'd already been through all this with my dad the previous day when I'd updated my parents on progress at the cottage. I'd carefully given Simon's side of the story and then explained Luke's response. I should have known Dad would immediately side with the builder over my fiancé, although to be fair, when he rationalised it to me I saw his point.

'The bloke's done this sort of thing for years, love, so I would think his opinion counts for a lot more than that of some reporter who can barely change a plug.'

'I think Simon just wants to see some signs of progress,' I explained. 'Right now, it doesn't look as if anything's happening, and I think he's worried that we're spending a lot of money on nothing.'

But, as Dad reasoned, Luke was taking steps to tackle the penetrating damp that plagued the cottage, and it was pointless doing anything until that had been dealt with.

I'd spoken to Luke that morning, querying what, exactly, he was doing, as Simon had been vague about it all. Luke wasn't in the least bit snappy or impatient with me, so it was better that I ask the questions rather than Simon.

'At the moment I'm repointing the brickwork,' he told me. 'At some point, the lime mortar's been replaced with cement, and that can contribute to dampness.'

I'd nodded, hoping I looked as if I understood the difference. 'And will that do the trick? I mean, will that solve the damp issues?'

Luke had pulled a face. 'Not entirely, no. The render wants repairing, too. I'm getting some of the roof tiles replaced and then I'll be tackling the guttering.' He surveyed me for a moment, a twinkle suddenly appearing in his dark, thickly fringed eyes. 'Sent you to check up on me, has he?'

I tried to sound convincing as I assured him that Simon trusted him implicitly and that I was merely asking out of interest.

'The thing is,' he said, 'if you don't get these basics dealt with first, you're just going to be wasting your money. No point putting a plaster over a burst artery, as they say.'

'Simon's just a bit—'

'Of a prat?'

He'd mumbled the words, but I was almost sure I'd heard correctly. Even so, I had to check. 'Sorry, what did you say?'

Luke shrugged. 'Me? I didn't say anything.' He smiled at me, and I thought what lovely teeth he had, and what a cheeky grin he possessed. Then I thought I really shouldn't be thinking such kind thoughts about a man who, I was certain, had just insulted my fiancé.

'As I was saying,' I said firmly, 'Simon's just a bit concerned about finances, that's all. He's, er, quite big on getting value for money.'

Luke's smile vanished. 'Ask anyone round here and they'll tell you I'm as honest as the day as is long. I've got a good reputation. A builder's nothing without that, and I hope he's not going to be casting aspersions about my honesty.'

'Oh no, nothing like that,' I assured him hastily. 'He'd never mean to offend you, I promise. We're just on a tight budget, that's all.'

Luke considered me for a moment, his head tilted slightly to one side. His dark curls shook as he finally shrugged and I thought what beautiful hair he had, all gypsy-like and romantic, and not at all like Simon's neat, respectable crop.

'Renovating old houses like this one can eat money,' Luke said at last. 'I know sometimes they seem like a real bargain when they come up for auction, but you've got to factor in the costs.'

'Well, obviously,' I said, rather indignantly. 'We're not stupid. We understood that.'

'And there must be some sort of contingency fund because unexpected problems can crop up. You know that?'

'Simon researched the whole thing very carefully before we proceeded,' I said. 'You don't have to worry about getting paid if that's what you're getting at.'

His brows knitted together rather masterfully as he growled, 'That wasn't what I meant at all, but thanks for clearing that up. Can I get back to work now? After all, time's money.'

Suitably chastened, I hurried away to assure Simon all was well, and Luke knew exactly what he was doing. He remained unconvinced.

That very morning they'd had an argument about the windows. Simon wanted to replace them with new ones, but Luke insisted that we'd be much better off repairing the ones that were already in place.

'It's not listed,' Simon had pointed out. 'I don't see why we have to go to all that trouble.'

Luke had rolled his eyes in a manner remarkably like my dad's and said patiently, as if explaining to a child, 'Because the more original features you can retain in a house like this, the more it will hold its value. That's why folk want these old places, you see? What's the point of buying a house this age then putting modern windows in if you can save the ones already here?'

Put like that he had a point, but Simon remained unconvinced. 'I think we should look at uPVC,' he said firmly. 'We're on the coast after all. Well, as good as.'

'What do you think, Katy?'

I'd shivered as Luke looked directly at me and used my name for the first time. It sounded terribly intimate, and I gaped at him, unable to reply.

Simon gave me a filthy look. 'Well?'

'Well what? Oh!' I blushed. 'Well, er, I think it would look lovely if we could repair the original windows and clean them up a bit.' Seeing his glare, I stammered, 'But then again, double glazing would be practical.'

Luke's expression softened as Simon tutted. 'You're no use whatsoever. We'll discuss this another time. We're heading home.' He'd glanced at his watch and said, 'I take it I can trust you to stay here until five?'

The softness in Luke's eyes vanished to be replaced by a cold, hard stare. 'I'm not in the habit of sneaking off early if that's what you're implying.'

'Hmm. Glad to hear it.'

Even I was appalled by Simon's rudeness. I gave Luke an apologetic smile and followed my clearly seething fiancé to the car.

As we sat together in the living room, plates of Chinese takeaway on our knees, I thought wearily that I'd be glad to get back to work for a rest. All this fighting for supremacy was exhausting. I could only hope things would improve.

'I'm aching everywhere,' I said. 'I need a nice hot bubble bath I think.'

'Mm.' Simon shovelled chop suey into his mouth and didn't even glance over at me. I remembered how he used to run me a bath whenever I was tired and achy, and how he'd fill the bathroom with scented candles and bring me up a glass of wine to enjoy while I soaked in the tub. He hadn't done that for such a long time.

When Cartwheel Cottage is finished and we move in, things will get back to normal, I thought. It was only the stress of the renovation project. Our home might need major repair work, but our relationship just needed time. Didn't it?

Chapter 5
God Rest Ye Merry, Gentlemen

My mobile was ringing. Cursing, I realised I needed to find a safe place to pull over, but in the darkness and with the snow falling heavily it wasn't that easy to see. By the time I'd found the layby that I'd been looking for the phone had stopped. I checked the missed calls list, to find Penny's name at the top. Now what?

'Oh, I've just rung you!'

Her voice was light and cheerful, and I could hear laughter and the sound of the television in the background. I felt a pang of regret that I wasn't spending Christmas with them. There would have been no time to brood or mope with Penny and Mike, that was certain.

'I know you've just rung me. That's why I called you back,' I said, rolling my eyes.

'Oh right. Of course. I was just ringing to see if you'd got home safely and ask how it's all going.'

I bit my lip, hating having to lie. 'Oh, yes. All's well. I'm just about to have a nice long soak in the bath. Dad's watching television and Mum's getting quietly sloshed in the kitchen on Snowballs, so I've decided to have a bit of peace while I can.'

'Oh, you lucky thing! I'd kill for five minutes alone in a bubble bath. It's murder here already. The kids are so excited about tomorrow; I doubt any of us will get any sleep tonight.'

I thought about the freezing caravan I was heading home to and decided I wasn't likely to get much sleep either. 'I don't envy you,' I said, lying through my teeth. 'Give me peace and quiet any day.'

'Oh well, I'd better get back to the kitchen. I've got a million things to do before I can go to bed anyway. Still haven't wrapped Mike's presents, so I've got to find time to do that yet, not to mention somewhere I won't be disturbed. It's all go. Are you having turkey? Mine's cooking right now. Smells gorgeous. It's making me so hungry I've already eaten five sausage rolls that were supposed to be for tomorrow.'

I forced myself to sound cheerful. 'Absolutely. A whopping big turkey. Far too much for three people. And mince pies, and Christmas cake and chocolates galore. I'll be a stone heavier when this is over.'

I thought about the microwave meal and the paltry half pound of Quality Street and felt like wailing down the phone, *help me, save me! This is going to be the worst Christmas ever. I'll sleep in the bath if I have to, just let me come back to yours. I don't want to be The Little Match Girl.*

Penny laughed, blissfully unaware of my misery. 'Me, too. Never mind. It's only once a year. Oh, sorry, Katy, must go. Mike's lost the bottle opener — major disaster! I'll call you tomorrow, okay? Wish your mum and dad a merry Christmas from me.'

'Sure will. Must dash, bath will be overflowing.'
'Ooh, enjoy! Merry Christmas.'
'Yeah, merry—'

But she was gone. I gazed tearfully at the blank screen for a moment, imagining the scene at her home. There'd be a lot of noise, no doubt, but a lot of laughter and good humour too. Plenty of food, plenty of drink, plenty of good company. No microwave turkey meals for the Miltons and their guests.

'Oh, get a grip for God's sake,' I muttered.

Checking the mirrors then over my shoulder for oncoming traffic, I indicated and moved slowly off. I needed to get home if you could call a knackered caravan home. As bleak as it was, it was still better than being stuck in a car in the middle of nowhere in thick snow.

***

Things hadn't improved between Luke and Simon. On the contrary, it seemed that Simon deliberately blocked anything Luke suggested and found fault in everything he did, delaying the work and making himself extremely unpopular with Luke's employees and the other workmen he'd sub-contracted.

I couldn't help thinking that some of Luke's ideas were much better than ours. He seemed to have an instinctive feeling for the property and knew exactly what would work. I found myself arguing with Simon more and more about how the finished cottage should look.

After some rather tiresome weeks of travelling backwards and forwards to Weltringham, Simon told me he had a surprise for me.

For a moment I foolishly wondered if he'd set a date for the wedding, but then realised how unlikely that was.

'Where are we going?' I asked as he led me to his car, practically beaming with delight. Clearly, whatever my surprise was, he was very pleased with himself about it.

We drove a few miles out of the city towards the market town of Beverley, and Simon was extremely annoying, refusing to tell me what was going on, despite my badgering. Eventually, we turned off the main road and down a winding lane.

'What is this place?' I stared glumly out of the window at the dozens of caravans parked on a large field, taking note of the shower block and wooden cabin that apparently was some sort of launderette. 'Surely we're not going on holiday here?'

'As if!' He laughed and I felt quite weak with relief. Communal showers and toilets were definitely not my thing.

'So, what are we doing here?' I said, feeling puzzled.

'Well, you know Mel at work?'

'Not really,' I admitted. He may have mentioned the name once or twice, but his stories were usually so deadly dull that my mind turned to other things mid-conversation most of the time.

'Of course you do. Married to Eric? They live near Driffield?'

'Umm, no…'

'He had that knee replacement last year and she took weeks off work to take care of him.'

'Oh,' I cried, 'that Mel!'

I still had no idea who he was talking about, but I knew from experience that we could play this game for ages if I didn't pretend to remember her.

'Yes, that's the one,' he agreed. 'Anyway, they had a holiday caravan out near Filey, but it had to be removed from the site because there's some clause in the contract that states no caravans more than ten years old can be sited there, so they had to get it towed here while they can sell it, you see.'

'Right.' I didn't understand his point. What did I care about Mel and Eric's ancient Filey caravan?

'You're not grasping this are you?' he said, in a most patronising tone. Honestly, I think he'd have patted me on the head if he hadn't been driving. 'Don't you see where I'm going with this?'

I frowned. 'Not really. Do you?'

'Katy, don't you understand? Mel has lent it to us — well, she's rented it to us, but at half the price we're paying for that poky little house we're currently living in.'

'You mean, we're going to be living *here*?' I could barely hide my horror.

'Don't be dense,' he said. 'It's going to be towed to the cottage and parked in the front garden. We can live in it while the work's completed. It will be much cheaper and, as a bonus, we'll be able to keep more of an eye on Luke Ingledew. No skiving off at four just because at least one of us isn't there to oversee him. Don't you think it's a marvellous idea?'

I tried to sound positive as we bumped along the track and I peered out at a variety of static caravans, some with verandas, and hoped for the best.

'Which one is it?' We'd nearly run out of field.

Luke tutted. 'None of these. These are rentals and holiday homes. Ours is in storage.' He pointed towards the windscreen. 'That big building over there, see? That's where it's being kept at the moment.'

When I finally clapped eyes on our future temporary home, I could see perfectly well why the holiday camp in Filey had decided that it needed to be removed from their site. Shabby didn't begin to cover it, and unlike the caravans we'd passed on our way to the glorified shed that it currently sat in, there was no sign of any double glazing either.

Mel, a cheerful blonde who was almost as wide as she was tall, kept telling us that she didn't mind doing us a favour, and anything for a friend, and she was only too glad she could help.

I couldn't help thinking that it was us doing *her* a favour. After all, rather than pay storage fees for the bloody thing she'd be getting weekly rent for it instead. Quite a good result for the generous Mel if you ask me.

Simon was clearly delighted that he'd solved our problems and I didn't like to burst his bubble, so I assured Mel we were very grateful and that we'd take care of her beloved caravan and tried not to cry as she and Simon discussed removal and re-siting with the owner of the storage place.

We gave a month's notice on the rental property, but Simon wanted to move to Weltringham as soon as possible, so it was two weeks later that we packed up and moved in, incurring not only rental costs for the caravan but also for a storage unit for our furniture and most of our personal belongings. I couldn't see there was much financial benefit to the move at all, and I suspected it was simply down to Simon's pathological mistrust of Luke and his determination to be on site as much as possible to keep an eye on him.

Indeed, Simon did seem happier for a while, secure in the knowledge that Luke was no longer able to bunk off work early (not that I thought for one second that he ever had) and certain that, at last, he could make sure that the work was being done to his taste and satisfaction.

***

I think the beginning of the end came when he got home one night to find Luke in the caravan with me.

It was all perfectly innocent. We were simply watching television and drinking tea. Simon was working late, and I'd arrived home alone to be greeted by a cheery call from the top of the scaffolding that surrounded Cartwheel Cottage. I glanced up, surprised to see Luke still working.

'What are you doing up there?' I shouted.

He waved. 'Just finishing now. Where's the boss?'

I shook my head at his sarcasm but grinned all the same. 'Working late. Do you want a cup of tea?'

He leaned on the scaffolding and pushed his hard hat back slightly, as if to get a better look at me. 'Are you sure? I don't know if that's in my contract, drinking with my betters.'

'Don't be cheeky,' I called. 'I'm putting the kettle on now so don't be long.'

Ten minutes later he knocked on the caravan door and I yelled, 'Come in,' over the sound of the kettle.

He opened the door and stepped inside, looking around him and wrinkling his nose before he noticed that I was watching him and forced a smile.

'Cosy isn't it?'

'You could say that.'

I glanced around at the stained carpet and the grubby fixed seating and sighed. 'At least it won't be for long. It *won't* be for long, will it?'

He took off his hard hat and grinned. 'Caravan life getting you down?'

'I wouldn't recommend it,' I admitted. 'Not long term anyway.'

'I'll do my best to hurry things along,' he promised.

'But you'll not cut corners.' It wasn't a question.

'Of course not.' He ran a hand through his untidy hair, looking wistful suddenly. 'Cartwheel Cottage deserves better than that. Whatever your — fiancé — thinks of me, I wouldn't do anything less than my best.'

'I know that, honestly.' I smiled and there was an awkward silence for a moment as he stared at me, and I wondered if he believed that I genuinely trusted him or thought I was just being polite. 'Sugar?'

The smile was back in place instantly, and I felt a flutter of delight at the sight of it. 'Yes, honey?'

'Idiot! I mean, do you take sugar?'

'Certainly not. I'm sweet enough.'

'I believe you.'

'I'm relieved to hear it. I thought you had me down as some sort of unscrupulous villain, out to rip you off and steal your money.'

'Of course not. Simon doesn't think that either,' I said, hoping he wouldn't hear the strained tone in my voice as I handed him his mug of tea.

He narrowed his eyes as he reached for the drink, and I realised I wasn't fooling him for an instant.

'If it's any consolation,' I said, 'I think I've persuaded Simon to stick with our old windows.'

His face lit up. 'Really? How did you manage that?' I blushed fiercely as he held up one hand and said hastily, 'You know what? Don't tell me. I really don't want to know.'

'He's a reasonable man when you get to know him,' I said, feeling unaccountably flustered. 'Biscuit?'

'No thanks. I really must get off when I've had this tea. Mum will be cooking as I speak.'

'Is it difficult, living back at home with your parents?' I asked. 'I don't think I could cope living with my mum and dad again.'

As it happened, I didn't have that option any longer. I'd only left the family home for what felt like ten minutes when they announced they were downsizing and planned to use the equity on the house to, as Dad put it, *have a bloody good time*.

'That was quick,' I'd gasped, stunned at the speed of their decision.

'You must be joking,' Dad said. 'We've had this planned for years. We've just been waiting for you to get your own place. Thought you'd taken root. You've been harder to shift than Japanese Knotweed.'

'Oh thanks, Dad,' I'd replied.

'Dave! Ignore him, Katy, it wasn't like that at all. You know we were happy to have you living with us as long as you wanted.'

Dad sighed. 'Calm down, Moira. She knows I'm kidding. Bloody hell. Did a good job that surgeon, didn't he, Katy?'

'What surgeon?' I asked, puzzled.

'The bugger who gave your mother that sense of humour bypass.'

'Oh, shut up,' Mum said, nudging him. She turned to me, her eyes full of anxiety. 'You don't really mind us moving, do you, love? Only, it seems silly to rattle around here when we could buy something smaller and free up some capital. You understand?'

Of course I understood, and I didn't blame them one little bit, but it did give me a pang when they left the large, semi-detached house I'd grown up in and moved to a two-bedroomed terraced cottage a couple of miles from our old home.

Within weeks, Dad had commandeered the smallest bedroom to accommodate his new hobby — making home brew. With all the barrels and bottles there was no room for me to even stay overnight, let alone move back in. Not that I'd want to move back in, obviously. I'd had a taste of freedom and couldn't imagine being back under their roof, as much as I loved them.

Luke clearly had no such qualms about living with his family. 'To be fair, they're so busy with the pub I don't see that much of them. They're good people. I've no complaints. Mind you, they might be getting a bit sick of seeing me. Thought they'd got rid of me for good, you see, yet I bounced back like the proverbial bad penny.'

'So you could save money for your next project.'

'That's right.'

'Have you got anything in mind?'

He was quiet for a moment, sipping his tea, then he shook his head. 'Not at the moment.'

'Just in case something comes up then?'

'Yeah, yeah. Just in case.'

I felt uncomfortable, as if something was nagging away at me but I couldn't work out what. I reached over and switched on the tiny television, desperate to break the silence. Luckily, my favourite quiz show was still on, and we spent a happy ten minutes trying to beat each other at answering the questions and laughing at the hapless contestants and the presenter's corny jokes.

When the caravan door flew open and Simon stepped inside, I think Luke was as shocked as I was. Mind you, I think Simon's shock was greater, judging by the expression on his face.

'Well, this is cosy,' he ground out, his eyes sparking with anger as he stared at an unflinching Luke. 'No work to do?'

I could have died of shame. I mean, how rude was that? Not to mention ridiculous.

'It's way past clocking off time,' I pointed out.

'No need to make excuses for me, Katy,' Luke said, standing up and putting his cup in the sink. 'I was just going, as it happens. Although,' he added, facing Simon, 'what I do in my own time is *my* business *and*, I think you'll find, I've been on my own time for well over an hour now, despite working late to finish something off for you.' He turned to give me a sympathetic smile. 'Thanks for the tea, Katy. See you tomorrow.'

The caravan door had barely closed before Simon banged his fist on the worktop and spat, 'That man! What the hell was he doing here, drinking my tea and watching my television?'

His tea! *His* television! I gave him a filthy look. 'He was just keeping me company. I invited him in, and I wasn't aware that I had to ask your permission to have friends round for a drink.'

'Friends! He's not a friend, for God's sake. He's — he's—'

'What? What is he, Simon? Staff? A servant?'

'Don't be ridiculous.'

'I'm not the one being ridiculous. You've just embarrassed me and embarrassed yourself. How could you be so rude to him?'

'I don't like him,' he muttered.

'You don't say? I'd never have guessed.'

'I don't want to come home from work and find that man in my home again, do you hear me?'

'And I don't want to have orders barked at me by my own fiancé as if he's my boss. Do *you* hear *me*?'

We glared at each other.

'Sod this,' he snapped. 'I'm going out.'

'You've only just come in,' I protested. 'You haven't even eaten.'

'There's a pub in the village. I'll eat there. And no,' he added, his eyes dark with fury, 'I don't mean the bloody Seagull Inn either. Wild horses wouldn't drag me in there. I'll try The Queen's Head and I'll bet it's a much better pub anyway.'

'Fine,' I said, suddenly too weary to argue any longer. 'Go then. I don't think I want your company this evening after all.'

Even so, I was quite surprised when he wrenched open the caravan door and headed outside, slamming the door behind him. So, he meant it. He was going to eat in the village.

I watched the caravan door for a minute or two, half-expecting him to return with a sheepish smile and an apology, but nothing happened.

Sighing, I turned to the little fridge and began to rummage around for something to eat, before giving it up as a bad job and slumping listlessly in front of the television again.

Suddenly, I was no longer hungry.

***

Things between Luke and Simon went from bad to worse after that. They clashed endlessly and I wasn't surprised when they decided to part company. It was the first thing they'd agreed on.

'Please don't go,' I begged Luke as he loaded up his van, his face grim. 'You understand this place so well and your ideas are perfect. Give it another chance.'

He shook his head and slammed the doors shut, then turned to me. I saw the expression in his eyes soften and he put his hand on my shoulder as I stood there, blinking back tears.

'I'm sorry, Katy,' he murmured. 'If I thought I could make a difference, if I thought for one moment that he'd listen…'

'I'll make him listen,' I said, though I had no idea how I planned to achieve that.

'How do you stand it? How do you stand *him*?'

For some unaccountable reason my face burned, and my stomach churned. Why, I wondered, did I suddenly feel so reluctant to defend my fiancé to Luke?

'Please,' I whispered. 'Stay. It won't be the same if you go. What will I — we — do without you?'

He looked down at the path for a moment, his teeth nipping his bottom lip, and I watched him, desperately hoping that my words would have the desired effect. Then he looked up and I saw the sadness in his face and knew I'd lost.

'It's too hard,' he murmured. 'I'm sorry. I can't stay here any longer.'

So he'd gone, and it wasn't long before Simon was cursing his actions as it proved impossible to find someone at such short notice to continue with the work. The weeks dragged on, and he eventually found someone who could take over, but at a vastly increased price and not until he'd finished another project.

It was another step closer to the end of my world…

Chapter 6
It's the Most Wonderful Time of the Year

I peered through the windscreen, my wipers moving rapidly to clear the glass as flurries of snow showered the car with alarming frequency. I shivered, thinking of the caravan. What fun it was going to be, tucked away in that tin can on wheels for a couple of days. The gas fire in the living room just about kept the worst of the chill off, but the bedroom would be freezing. It always was — especially since I'd slept in there alone.

I'd called Luke the week before to warn him I was spending Christmas in Weltringham and to ask if he'd mind putting on the caravan light and the fire before I got there.

'What time will you be here?' he'd asked.

'Around half past five, I should think,' I'd said, somewhat optimistically as it turned out.

Weltringham looked so pretty as I arrived at the main street that it brought a lump to my throat.

All Saints' Church dominated the village, standing on raised ground with a high cobbled wall surrounding it. In the spring the church yard was a mass of daffodils. Now, the gravestones were shrouded in snow, but it still looked beautiful, light shining through the stained-glass windows of the church as preparations continued for the carol concert that was due to take place any time now.

I could see people spilling out of The Seagull Inn, already looking the worse for wear. I wondered if Luke was in there. I hoped he'd remembered to put the fire on for me. In all likelihood he'd be with his workmates, getting well and truly blotto. Well, I couldn't blame them. In other circumstances I'd be doing the same.

I imagined Mum and Dad on their cruise ship and smiled briefly. Mum would be in her element, no doubt. Dad, on the other hand, would be longing to change out of his smart clothes and put his old jogging bottoms on. He'd be missing his favourite Christmas telly programmes too. I hoped they supplied tins of Roses and boxes of After Eights on that ship. It just wouldn't feel like Christmas to Dad if not.

I wondered briefly what Simon was doing. Probably still working if I knew him. Not that I did know him — not the way I'd thought anyway. The Simon I knew would never have called off our engagement, throwing all our plans and dreams away for the sake of promotion and the chance to move to London.

I mean, London! What happened to our vision of country life, of a cottage by the sea? When it came right down to it, Weltringham couldn't compete with a huge salary increase and a swish flat in the capital which he was going to share with some colleagues.

***

It had come out of the blue as far as I was concerned, though looking back, I suppose there had been warning signs.

Simon had started picking faults in Weltringham. The pretty little village he'd fallen in love with had suddenly seemed to irritate him.

He didn't like The Queen's Head, saying it was too basic and lacked the sort of facilities that modern pubs should have. What he meant was it was full of locals and the locals hadn't really taken to him. Not surprising. Luke's family may have run a rival pub, but the village was a small one. Everyone knew each other and defended each other against outsiders, and like it or not, my fiancé and I were still very much outsiders.

I'd ventured into The Queen's Head once or twice with Simon, and you could cut the atmosphere with a knife. Some of the customers nodded and smiled at me, but backs were turned when Simon approached, and I must admit, it seemed to take an awfully long time for him to get served at the bar. I wasn't surprised when he stopped going in there.

Of course, The Seagull Inn was totally out of bounds as far as he was concerned, so if we wanted an evening out it meant a drive to the next village. Even there, we faced suspicious looks and could hear low mutterings of disapproval. We weren't imagining it. Evidently, Luke's family had connections throughout Holderness.

Simon also started to moan about not having a supermarket on the doorstep. There was a local shop, but he complained that it was overpriced and didn't carry enough variety of stock.

We'd popped in one evening on the way home from work, having decided to cook a proper meal for a change, and Simon had been outraged by the fact that the food we needed could be bought for much less in the supermarket near work.

'Why should we pay all that for a packet of mince?' he demanded. 'It's a rip-off.'

'Shh,' I whispered, all too aware that it was a small shop, and the other customers could probably hear every word. 'You know local shops have to charge more. They can't buy in bulk like supermarkets. For goodness' sake, what's wrong with you?'

'We should have called at Asda on the way home,' he grumbled.

'Well, we would have done if we'd decided to cook earlier, but we only thought of it ten minutes ago so—'

'If we had a freezer it would help. We could stock up every week instead of being reliant on this dump.'

'Simon!' I was mortified and edged away from him, as if I could convince everyone I wasn't with him. I glanced over at the counter where Yesoob, who ran the shop, was clearly pretending not to hear. He was a lovely, kindly man, who always had a twinkle in his eye and a friendly smile on his face. He'd done nothing to deserve Simon's rudeness.

I glared at my fiancé. This shop might not be as cheap or as well-stocked as a supermarket, but it was warm and friendly, and Yesoob always had time to chat and unfailingly remembered my name without any prompting. It was one of the many things we'd loved about the village — having that level of personal service and a connection with local people. What on earth was wrong with Simon?

Anyway, whose fault was it that we didn't have a freezer? Whose bright idea had it been to give up our rented house and move into that horrible caravan anyway? In fact, whose idea was it to move to Weltringham in the first place?

The occasional grumble turned into constant moaning. Simon would pick fault in everything to do with the village. Eventually, he started picking faults in me too. Nothing I did was right and living in such a confined space didn't help. We were falling over each other, and the arguments became frequent and more heated.

Even so, I was *not* expecting the bombshell when it arrived, and I had to sit down as Simon broke the news to me.

'Let's face it,' he'd said, trying to be as gentle as he could, 'things haven't been right for a long time. You must have felt it too? We've drifted apart. I don't know, maybe it was just the pressure of this place. We took on too much, don't you think? It was a stupid dream.'

'But it was *our* dream,' I'd protested, choking on tears. 'We were going to make it beautiful again and live here and start a family.'

He shook his head. 'I'm sorry, Katy, honestly. I just don't think we thought it through properly. It was a mad idea. I've been really stressed and tired trying to make it work, but in the end I had to be honest with myself. When this job came up, I knew I had to go for it. Think of it. A reporter on national television! I know I'll start with minor stories but think what it could lead to. This is my big chance, Katy. It's what I've always wanted.'

'Funny that because I thought *I* was what you'd always wanted.'

Even as I said the words, though, I realised it wasn't true. I'd never really believed I was the love of Simon's life. There'd always been that nagging feeling that things weren't right between us. Why hadn't I paid attention to my doubts?

Dad, it seemed, had been right all along. He was insistent that Simon's repeated postponement of our wedding meant it didn't really matter to him; that *I* didn't matter to him. I hadn't wanted to believe it, so I'd hung onto Mum's scornful denials and believed her when she said Simon was just being sensible and responsible — qualities that would make him the perfect husband. So much for that.

'So, what about me?' I murmured. 'What do I do now?'

'I wouldn't dream of asking you to move to London,' he replied. 'I know you'd hate it. You'll find the right person one day and when you do, you'll find the right home too.'

How easily he said those words, as if it didn't matter to him in the slightest if I found someone else. I'd been such a fool.

'And what about the cottage? What do I do about that now?'

'I emailed Ingledew. I told him I won't be onsite in the future and that he'll be answering to you from now on. I didn't go into any details, but he seemed happy to come back once he knew that.'

I gasped. 'You did what? After everything you said about him?' The hypocrisy stunned me, and he had the grace to look sheepish.

'Yeah, well, I thought there was no point paying the exorbitant prices of that other builder, and we never signed anything, after all. Once Ingledew has finished the work we'll sell the cottage. I'll need all the cash I can get for living in London, and we should make a good profit when it's done. It will give you some capital to invest in your own place too. It will work out better for both of us. We'll put it on the market the other side of

Christmas. House sales pick up then. It's for the best, you'll see.'

I failed to see how. Cartwheel Cottage was my dream home and now I was going to lose it before I'd even lived there. There would never be wedding photos of Simon and me and our children on a chunky oak sideboard now. There'd be no happy family Christmases; no scruffy dog playing chase with fair-haired boys and girls who looked just like their daddy. One day, this house might ring with laughter once again, but it wouldn't be my laughter. I would only know Cartwheel Cottage as an empty shell.

I grieved for everything I'd dreamed of having. Perhaps I grieved more for what might have been than for the man I supposedly loved.

I'd stayed on at the caravan for a few weeks, trying to stay cheerful, trying to remain positive, but I felt lost and afraid. The only bright spot on the horizon was the return of Luke. My heart leapt when he knocked on the caravan door early one morning, a smile on his face and a twinkle in those dark eyes.

'Bit of a turn-up for the books, isn't it?' he said. 'I was amazed when your fiancé rang me and offered me the job back. When he said he wouldn't be onsite to interfere any more… I'm guessing he's got some big project on at work? Something to distract him from Cartwheel Cottage? No doubt he's left me a mountain of instructions though.'

His smile dropped when I listlessly told him to do whatever he wanted to the place. Obviously, we had to stay within the plans, but the fixtures and fittings were up to him. I saw no point in creating a dream home that I'd have to leave very soon.

'I don't understand.'

'Simon's no longer a part of this,' I said, trying to keep my voice steady. 'Our engagement's over.'

'You broke it off?'

'I didn't, no. Something better came along. London and a better job, to be precise.'

He stared at me, apparently as shocked as I was that Simon had called off our engagement. 'I can't believe it. How could he bear to…? He must be mad!'

'I know,' I said. 'Who'd swap Weltringham for London? I just don't understand it.'

He seemed about to say something but then shook his head, turned to look at the cottage and considered for a moment. 'I'm so sorry, Katy. I know how much this place means to you. It's a crying shame. It used to be so beautiful, and it will be again, I promise you. I'll create the perfect home for you.'

'It doesn't really matter,' I'd sniffed. 'I've got to sell it anyway. Simon wants his share back and I can't afford to buy him out. I'll never live here now. It was all a waste of time.'

He half reached out to me but seemed to change his mind. His arm dropped to his side, and he looked at me with sad, dark eyes. 'You would have been happy here, I know it. I only came back here because I wanted to see the renovation through. It wasn't for Simon, that's for sure. If it had been any other job he could have begged and pleaded until the twelfth of never and I'd still have said no, but I've loved this house since I was a child. I wanted it myself; did you know that? As a home, I mean, not a project. You outbid me sadly.'

I gazed up at him. 'This cottage? This was the project you sold your home and moved back in with your parents for? Oh, Luke, I'm so sorry.'

'Don't be.' He shrugged. 'Everything happens for a reason, or so my mother's always telling me. I'll admit, I was gutted to lose it, but I've loved working on it. It's been a privilege to bring new life to the place. Whatever happens, you can be proud that you've helped bring that about.'

I tried to be noble about it but all I could think was that I was going to lose the home that I loved so much already.

***

Mum and Dad hadn't liked me living all alone in the caravan.

'If only we'd known,' Mum wailed. 'I'd never have let your father talk me into downsizing.'

Dad gaped at her, and I shook my head slightly, all too aware that it had been Mum who'd been the driving force behind their move.

'I can clear out that spare bedroom,' Dad had promised me. 'Daft bloody idea anyway, home brew.'

'Don't give me that,' I'd said, laughing. 'I know you're enjoying it. Very proud of your beer, aren't you?'

He was too. He'd tried several different varieties and had decided he was a gifted brewer who'd missed his vocation.

'Should have bought a micro-brewery years ago,' he told me gloomily. 'Reckon I'd be a millionaire now.'

Simon hadn't appreciated his efforts, though Dad had perversely insisted he try every new variety. He'd pulled a face and rolled his eyes at me every time Dad told him about his latest brew and urged him to taste it.

'For God's sake,' he'd groaned at me as we'd driven home one night, 'why does he insist on making me drink that disgusting concoction?'

'Isn't it any good?' I'd asked, having never tasted any of Dad's creations, not being a beer lover.

'It's enough to strip the hairs from your nostrils,' Simon groaned. 'He should bottle it as a toilet cleaner or something. That's all it's good for, trust me.'

Funnily enough, Luke didn't share his opinion.

Mum and Dad had driven down to Weltringham one evening, bringing me fish and chips and a bottle of wine, along with half a dozen bottles of home brew for *that nice builder who's been so good to you.*

I really hadn't wanted to give them to Luke, since his parents were, after all, in the trade, and having seen Simon's reaction to Dad's gifts, I was certain Luke would be equally, if not more, disparaging.

On the contrary, he thanked Dad profusely. He'd been called over by my parents after he'd packed up his van and had seemed quite touched when Dad offered the bottles to him.

'That's really thoughtful of you. Thank you very much.'

'Not at all, not at all,' Dad said. 'We really appreciate how hard you're working to get this place finished, and we know you put up with a lot from that nasty bugger she was hooked up with before.'

Luke flashed me a sympathetic look through the open caravan door as I blushed fiercely.

'Tell you what,' Dad suggested, 'why don't you come in and try them now?'

'Well, er, the van—'

'Katy tells me you only live up the road. You can leave your van here tonight and walk home, can't you?

Come on, I'd love to see what you think to them, you being a professional, so to speak.'

'Not me,' Luke said, shaking his head. 'It's my parents who are in the brewery business.'

'Well, even so.' Dad hooked his arm around Luke's shoulders. 'Come on, mate. I want to know what you think. No fibbing, mind. I want the gospel honest truth.'

Luke shrugged and climbed the caravan steps, whereupon Mum immediately pounced, pulling him into a seat next to hers and fussing over him as she passed him a bottle opener and a glass, even though Dad wanted him to drink straight from the bottle.

'Well?' Dad asked eagerly, as Luke wiped the back of his mouth and stared at what remained of his beer.

I hardly dare look at him, waiting for the forced compliment and half-hearted assurances that of course the beer was good.

Luke raised his glass at Dad. 'That's bloody good stuff, Mr Gillan,' he said, with evident enthusiasm. 'Best home brew I've ever tasted. I reckon it could beat some of the beers our pub serves into a cocked hat. Cheers.'

He'd eagerly taken another long gulp, and my eyes widened as I realised that he genuinely meant what he'd said.

Dad was beside himself with joy of course, and from then on, whenever I saw or heard from my parents, they always asked how *that smashing builder* was doing.

Chapter 7
Baby, it's Cold Outside

I drove slowly down the main street, passing a group of men who were laughing and serenading the world with a disrespectful version of While Shepherds Watched Their Flocks. I guessed they were on their way to The Queen's Head. I was almost certain some of them were Luke's employees.

I peered as closely as I could at them as I passed, but I couldn't see any sign of him. He was probably working behind the bar at his parents' pub. It would be very busy in The Seagull Inn, and he was just the sort of person who'd offer to help.

Children were coming out of the general store, and I couldn't help but smile at their excited faces. Christmas, after all, is made for children. I saw them waving goodbye to Yesoob.

There were crowds of villagers heading past me towards the church and I realised the carol service must be starting very soon. I wondered briefly if I should attend but decided that all those happy souls singing carols may be too much for me to bear. The only way I was going to get through the next two days was to lock myself in the caravan, eat lots of chocolate and immerse myself in my favourite television programmes. It would soon be over, and I'd be returning to Penny's before I knew it. Mike was right. The other side of Christmas was just a James Bond film away.

I felt panic rising as I realised suddenly that getting through Christmas was far from my biggest problem. It was, after all, what lay on the other side of it that frightened me the most. I felt cold with dread and, as I turned down the lane that led to Cartwheel Cottage, I wondered if I should have bought a big fat bottle of whisky too.

***

The move to Penny and Mike's had been their idea, not mine, but I can't pretend that I didn't bite their hand off at the suggestion.

As the weeks went by, living in the caravan all alone had become even more difficult. The two-storey extension to the cottage was finished and the original building was now waterproof and damp-free, but there was still no electricity, we needed a new boiler and central heating system, and we were in the process of repairing the windows. It was a long way from being ready to move into, thanks to all those weeks with no builders, and I was getting seriously depressed as the nights started to draw in and the weather turned colder.

Luke tried everything he could to cheer me up. While out walking Pip, he would often call in during the long, lonely evenings, to bring me something: flowers to brighten up the caravan, a flask of soup from the pub, a DVD player and some DVDs he thought I might enjoy, a book his mum had read which she thought would be just my cup of tea.

He showed me the plans he had for the kitchen and started coming up with designs for the garden.

Now that Simon wasn't on the scene to push him around and bark orders at him, he was eager to show me what he'd visualised for the cottage when buying it had been his own dream. I loved his ideas. I could really picture the cottage looking beautiful when it was done.

Simon had wanted a modern, contemporary design and we'd argued many times as I thought a more traditional look would suit Cartwheel Cottage. Luke showed me pictures of pretty country kitchens and suggested a stable door instead of the double-glazed one that Simon had decided on, and a gorgeous range rather than the stainless-steel built-in oven and hob that we'd circled in one of the manufacturers' catalogues.

He'd taken me to The Seagull Inn one evening after work. I think he felt sorry for me. The nights were getting dark, and the weather was on the turn. It was quite chilly in that tin can and the pub was warm and cosy with a welcoming atmosphere.

'You can't live on microwave meals,' he'd said, ignoring my protests and handing me a menu. The dining room was packed. A large, square room with an inglenook fireplace and cosy lamps on the walls, it was welcoming and warm. The menu was basic but, judging by the enthusiastic way my fellow diners were tucking in, the food was good.

Luke introduced me to his parents, and they greeted me like an old friend. Mrs Ingledew, small and plump with chestnut hair and large green eyes pulled me into a hug as if she'd known me all my life, and Mr Ingledew shook my hand warmly. He was tall and dark like his son, and I knew they were the sort of people who would buy Luke an engagement card should he ever propose to some lucky woman, unlike Simon's cold fish parents.

Despite my protests, they wouldn't hear of accepting payment for the meals. I was terribly grateful but couldn't help wishing I hadn't had a pudding after all. I'd have gone for the cheapest thing on the menu if I'd known.

Appetites sated, Luke and I sat together, our heads almost touching as we pored over the drawings he'd come up with for the garden. I admired the lay-out he'd designed, picturing the bushes and flowers and the patio and all the other wonderful features he'd thought of.

'I did a similar sort of thing for my sister at her house,' he told me.

'You have a sister?'

'Yes, her name's Victoria. I always make sure everyone knows she's three years older than me, because she hates that.' He grinned. 'She lives in the next village. I helped them renovate the place when they got married, and it's fantastic now. I'd like to take you there one day so you can see it for yourself. Of course, it's not exactly a show home, but she's got three kids, so what can you expect?'

He laughed and I thought, *I'll bet he's a wonderful uncle.*

'Three kids? Boys or girls?' I asked, wanting to know more about him. His parents were so lovely I was pretty sure his sister must be nice too. I really would like to meet her one day.

'Two boys and a girl,' he said, and I saw the softness in his eyes and heard the fondness in his tone and knew I'd been right to imagine he'd be a good uncle. 'A real handful, mind you, especially the youngest two. There's only a year between them and they get up to all sorts of mischief. Drive my sister to distraction. The eldest one's quieter. He's a reader and a thinker, like his dad. They're all lovely kids.'

I caught the wistful tone in his voice. 'Would you like kids of your own one day?'

He smiled. 'Nothing I'd like more. I always imagined a house full of them. Me, some imaginary wife, Pip, and sons and daughters running us all ragged. Funny really, I always pictured them in the garden of Cartwheel Cottage. Guess that's never going to happen now.'

I stared at him and watched as his cheeks flushed pink. I could feel my own face burning but I couldn't let the reason for it become more than a vague feeling. If I started to analyse it…

'The garden looks lovely,' I said hurriedly. 'On the plans I mean. I wish — I wish I could see it when it's all done, and the flowers are in full bloom. It's horrible to think I'll never know…'

I gulped as emotion got the better of me. Luke apologised immediately.

'I'm being very tactless. I'll put these away,' he said rolling up the drawings and securing them with an elastic band.

'It's okay. It's not your fault. I'm probably just overreacting because I haven't felt this warm or eaten such a good meal for ages.' I managed a smile, desperate to reassure him. 'I can see the place means as much to you as it does to me. Why don't you put in an offer for it when it goes up for sale?' I asked, my spirits sinking as I realised that the day was coming when the estate agent's board would go up in the front garden and Cartwheel Cottage would be nothing to do with me any longer. Christmas cards had started to appear in the shops. All that lay on the other side of Christmas was a big, black hole, where all my hopes and dreams would be buried.

He gave a half-laugh. 'You must be joking! I won't be able to afford it when it's finished. It will be well out of my price range. My own fault, I'm making it far too desirable. I should start doing some dodgy work on the place, bring the price right down.'

I got the feeling he was almost as sad as I was about the forthcoming sale and found myself wishing he'd outbid us after all. He deserved to own Cartwheel Cottage. He'd loved it for years and would have restored it sympathetically, lived in it happily, and never abandoned it for some swanky flat in London.

As October turned to November living in the caravan became unbearable. Luke watched me with worried eyes as I pulled into the drive one night, my shoulders hunched against the cold night air.

'What are you still doing here?' I asked him. He should have clocked off an hour ago.

'I'm taking you to the pub,' he replied. 'Mum's got a hot meal waiting for you and a big mug of hot chocolate with marshmallows that's got your name on it.'

I was too tired to protest and climbed into the van, leaned back in the seat, and almost fell asleep as he drove me to The Seagull Inn.

Mrs Ingledew was all sympathy and enveloped me in a massive hug as I walked in.

'Tomato soup to start with,' she said, 'then a nice roast dinner. Then I think,' she added as Luke helped me out of my coat, 'we should talk about you staying here till the work's done on that cottage.'

I shook my head. 'It's very kind of you, honestly, but—'

'I won't have any arguments,' she said, holding up her hand to silence me. 'Luke's worried sick about you and I'm not having my boy worrying, not when I can do something to prevent it. We've got a spare room and you're more than welcome.'

'But really—'

'You can't argue with Mum,' Luke told me, laughing. He took my hand and led me to a chair by the roaring fire. 'Sit down and eat your soup. Let us take care of you. It will be our pleasure.'

They were so kind. I had no idea why they were so good to me, especially given all the trouble Simon had caused for Luke, but they didn't understand.

'The thing is,' I explained, after a few mouthfuls of tomato soup had defrosted me enough to enable me to hold a proper conversation, 'I've already got somewhere to stay. My friend Penny has asked me to move in with her and her husband.'

Asked me? To be fair, she'd practically ordered me.

'Me and Mike have been talking it over and we can't stand the thought of you living in that bloody shed on wheels any longer. It's freezing now. We cranked the central heating up last night and we were both sitting there, worrying about you and how you were coping, with nothing between you and frostbite except that one poxy gas fire.'

I'd tried to assure her that I was perfectly fine but, evidently, I wasn't that good a liar.

'You'll have your own room,' she promised me. 'Just think of it, Katy. Radiators! A nice hot bath whenever you want one. And no more long drives home in the dark. Come on, you know you want to.'

'But won't Mike mind?' I'd asked, overcome at the picture of warmth and comfort that she'd painted and trying desperately not to fall on my knees in gratitude.

'It was Mike who told me to ask you,' she assured me. 'And the kids are beside themselves. Don't worry,' she added hastily. 'They won't bug you. Well, not too much. They're just really excited at the thought of you staying with us. Come on, Katy, say you will. I can't sleep for worrying and it's giving me bags under my eyes. You wouldn't want to be responsible for turning your best mate into an old hag, would you?'

I'd laughed, as much from sheer relief as anything, and had thanked her profusely for bailing me out of such a miserable situation. So, as lovely as it was of the Ingledews to offer, I was already sorted, and living with Mike and Penny made much more sense than moving to The Seagull Inn, which would still mean a long drive home every evening.

'They only live ten minutes from work so it's ideal. It's really good of you but, you see, there's no need to bother you at all. I'm sorted.'

Mrs Ingledew glanced across at Luke who was standing quite still, staring into the fire.

'So, how often do you think you'll come back to the cottage?' he murmured eventually.

I swallowed a chunk of crusty bread and took a sip of my hot chocolate. 'Not often,' I admitted. He turned to look at me and I sighed. 'The truth is, it's too painful being there now that I know it's got to be sold. I don't really want to see it anymore.'

'But we're so close to the finishing line,' he said, his eyes pleading. 'It won't be much longer. Surely you want to see how it all works out?'

'I trust your judgment,' I said wearily. 'Just get on with it the way you think best. Before you know it, it will be the other side of Christmas. I need to focus on the future. I'm sorry.'

We'd eaten our meal in silence, and he'd driven me home to the caravan, lit the fire for me and wished me goodnight before he drove off, leaving me with a lingering sense of guilt and a strange feeling of regret.

I'd moved to Penny's the next evening and hadn't been back to Weltringham since. I'd had a few stilted conversations with Luke on the telephone as he informed me of purchases made and work completed. He asked me how I was doing and if I'd heard from Simon, and I told him I was fine and that the only contact I'd had from Simon was a recommendation for an estate agent he knew; some friend of his who would do everything he could to ensure a quick sale. Luke was silent. There didn't seem much to say. I hadn't called again until the week before Christmas Eve, when I'd informed him I was coming back.

I'd made the decision to ignore the way my stomach fluttered at the sound of his voice. Life was complicated enough. I'd already lost my fiancé and was about to lose my beloved cottage; I couldn't deal with losing anything else. The truth was, I had an awful feeling that, if I allowed my emotions to get the better of me, that particular loss could be the most painful of them all.

Chapter 8
I'll Be Home for Christmas

Finally, weak with relief, I turned up the lane and drove towards Cartwheel Cottage. The snow had stopped falling, but the ground was crunchy beneath my feet as I climbed out of the car and took the bag of shopping from the back seat.

I glanced over at the cottage, which was in darkness, but at least I knew from Luke's updates that the electrical works were complete. The new boiler and central heating system were due to be installed in January. It was all coming together at last.

My heart sank as it dawned on me that the cottage wasn't the only place in darkness. The caravan light wasn't on either. With a heavy heart I trudged over to my temporary home. I fumbled in my pocket for my key and almost dropped it as my fingers were so numb with cold.

After several futile attempts, I managed to unlock the caravan door at last and it swung open. I peered nervously into the darkness. My heart sank. The fire wasn't lit either. The air inside the caravan felt as cold as the air outside. It was going to take ages to warm up. Luke has obviously forgotten all about it. About me.

I felt ridiculously disappointed in him and found myself suddenly close to tears. He'd *promised* me. I'd honestly believed that he was a man of his word but, clearly, I wasn't high up enough on his list of priorities. Why should he remember me after all?

I was about to flick the light switch when hands covered my eyes and I felt someone's breath on my neck. I was on the verge of screaming when I caught that fresh, spicy scent that I'd grown so familiar with, and recognition strangled the sound before it left my lips.

'Did you know it was me?' Luke said, letting me go. I switched on the light and turned to face him. He was standing on the caravan steps, smiling at me, and I was honestly tempted to push him off. Behind him I could see Pip peering up at me. I swear that dog was smiling.

I dropped the bag of shopping on the floor and glared at Luke.

'You forgot to put the fire on,' I said accusingly.

I gulped, horrified to hear the catch in my voice. What on earth was the matter with me? I blinked away tears and stared at him, hating him for standing there all happy and handsome, not caring at all that I'd had a journey from hell or that the highlight of my next forty-eight hours would be a frozen turkey platter and half a pound of Quality Street.

The expression in his eyes softened, and I was forced to acknowledge that I didn't hate him at all, and that, truthfully, that was a major part of the problem.

'I didn't forget, Katy,' he said, holding out his hand. 'I'd never forget anything you asked of me. Come with me.'

Reluctantly I took his hand, and he led me down the steps. I shut the caravan door after me, although it occurred to me that it wouldn't make much difference and, really, I ought to have stopped to light the fire at least, because it was going to be freezing when I got back.

As Luke led me to the front door of the cottage, I noticed for the first time that there was a wisp of smoke coming from the chimney. I stared at it for a moment then at him. He smiled and shook his head.

'You have to close your eyes,' he told me as we reached the doorstep. My heart thumped in anticipation, but I obeyed him, shivering as I heard the rattle of his keys and the creak of the door as it opened.

He led me inside and warmth seeped through my bones immediately. I slumped with pleasure, feeling my body start to thaw as I stood in the hallway, eyes firmly closed. I heard him close the door behind us, then he took my arm, and we walked forward. I heard another door being pushed open, the crackle of flames. I sniffed, catching the welcoming scent of woodsmoke.

'Okay. You can open them now,' he whispered in my ear.

I opened my eyes and gasped. The once crumbling old fireplace had been fully restored, and logs burned merrily in a brand-new wood burning stove. In the corner of the room stood a huge Christmas tree, beautifully decorated, and lit with dozens of fairy lights. Cranberry-scented candles burned in little pots on the mantelpiece and the hearth. The television from the caravan was on a small table and there was a battered leather sofa by the side of the fire. I looked at it enquiringly.

'It's mine, from my old place,' Luke explained. 'It's pretty old but it will do for now.'

I couldn't speak, overwhelmed with the surprise and delight of it all. Luckily, Luke didn't seem to expect me to talk.

He led me into the kitchen, flicking on the light. The kettle, toaster and microwave from the caravan were standing on a white plastic garden table which had four matching chairs tucked under it. All around the edges of the room were huge boxes. I could see from the drawings on the front of them that I had a new dishwasher, range cooker, fridge freezer and washing machine. The shabby old door had been replaced with a gorgeous wooden stable door and there were beautiful slate tiles on the floor.

'The kitchen will be fitted by the middle of January,' Luke promised. 'It's all in hand. After that, there's only the painting left to do. Do you want to see the bathroom?'

I nodded, unable to find the words, and he led me upstairs to show me a large family bathroom that was completely unrecognisable. I stared at the new suite and gorgeous shower in awe. Then I looked at him, puzzled.

'It's really warm up here. You said the central heating system was getting put in after Christmas.'

He smiled. 'I wanted to surprise you. As soon as I knew you were coming back for Christmas I called in a few favours. I couldn't have you staying in that damn caravan any longer. Have you any idea how unhappy it made me, seeing you stuck in that thing? There was no way I was going to let you spend Christmas in it.'

I wanted to ask him, why? What did it matter to him? But I couldn't bring myself to say the words. I suppose I didn't want to be disappointed if he didn't give me the answer I needed to hear.

'I really don't know what to say.'

He folded his arms and I realised he was nervous. He had no reason to be. From what I'd seen so far, the cottage was exactly as I'd wished it to be. He couldn't have done a better job. I gazed at him, trying to convey how wonderful the place was and how grateful to him I felt. He glanced down, looking awkward, then gave a half laugh.

'Come and look at your room,' he said, turning away from me and heading across the landing. I trembled as I followed him, wondering what I would find next.

'Oh!'

The bedroom walls were freshly plastered, and Luke had put a huge rug on the floor to cover the floorboards. Pip barked and ran past us, taking a flying leap onto a huge king-size bed in the middle of the room, where he settled quite comfortably as if it had been put there just for him.

I raised an eyebrow, my heart thumping.

'Where did that come from?'

He looked embarrassed. 'It's mine. Sorry about Pip; he clearly recognises it. Don't worry,' he said, holding up his hands, 'Mum's got an inflatable mattress at home that I can use. I just wanted you to be comfortable while you were here. Do you like it? The en suite's all done, too. I'm sorry about the kitchen. I really wanted it to be ready for you but there was no way it could be done on time, but we can make hot drinks and toast, and you're invited to the pub for Christmas dinner. Don't even think about saying no. Mum and Dad insist. *I* insist.'

'Do you?' I stared up at him, realising he was gabbling and that nerves had well and truly got the better of him.

Why had he gone to so much trouble for me? I knew the cottage meant a lot to him but there was no need for him to worry about making me comfortable. I wasn't his concern. Was I?

He smiled down at me as his fingers gently brushed away a lock of my hair that had fallen across my face. I took hold of his hand and he paused. My stomach churned with nerves, but I had to know. I had to ask the question.

'Why?' I murmured. 'Why would you do all this for me?'

For a long moment he simply stared at me, and I saw a million emotions flit across his face. He hesitated then he cupped my face and lowered his head until his lips met mine.

I've heard the expression, *time stood still*, many times, and I've always thought it was a huge exaggeration. No one can really feel like that, can they? But that was exactly how it felt, as we stood together, arms around each other, as if time had stopped. At one point I thought, maybe my heart was in danger of stopping too. I'd certainly never felt anything like it before. Simon's touch had never done that to me. His kiss had never made me feel the way Luke's was making me feel right now.

Loving, tender, it didn't last nearly long enough. I wanted more. So much more.

He looked at me, his eyes searching.

'Does that answer your question?' he asked gently, and I realised it did. In that moment, I understood, all too well, why he'd worked so hard to make things perfect for me.

'If you still want to sell up that's fine,' he said, his hands stroking my hair as he held me to him, his voice soft with love and warmth and kindness. 'Just know this; wherever you choose to live, I'll be willing to call it home, too. If you want to stay in the city, I'll move to the city. I love Cartwheel Cottage, but I love you more. I can't be without you, Katy. Tell me you feel the same.'

I didn't intend to smile, but my lips curved upwards of their own accord. Did I feel the same? *Oh, my darling, darling Luke, you have no idea.*

I put my arms around his neck and tilted my face towards his, and he pressed his lips to mine once more, this time with a passion that left us both breathless. I told him exactly how I felt without having to use a single word. Who needed conversation when it was so much nicer to kiss?

In the back of my mind, it occurred to me that Luke could probably afford to buy Simon's half of the cottage, and half of the cottage was all he would ever need.

It also occurred to me that it would be extremely rude to expect him to go all the way back to The Seagull Inn, to sleep on a lonely inflatable mattress, when there was that lovely, cosy king-size bed just standing there, practically inviting us in, something I finally pointed out to him when we'd stopped kissing long enough for me to get the words out.

Pip gave a joyful bark as Luke picked me up and swung me round, and we laughed as he leapt off the bed and circled us, tail wagging furiously.

Then Luke kissed me again and I knew that everything was going to be all right after all. I had a man I truly loved, who loved me in return.

One day, this cottage would ring with the laughter of dark-haired children who looked just like their daddy. Pip would chase them round the garden, and there would be cosy family Christmases and happy summer days soaked in sunshine and love. It all lay ahead of us; a promise, shining like gold, of wonderful days to come.

I could hardly wait for the other side of Christmas.

To find out more about Sharon Booth and her books visit her website

www.sharonbooth.com

where you can also sign up for her monthly newsletter to get her latest news, cover reveals, release dates, giveaways and more.

Also in the Home for Christmas series

Baxter's Christmas Wish

All Baxter wants is a good home and someone to love. He's not the only one.
When Ellie Jackson's marriage unexpectedly ends, she and her young son, Jake, seek refuge with Ellie's cousin, Maddie. But Maddie soon tires of her house guests, including her own boisterous rescue Boxer dog, Baxter.

A trip to the park proves eventful when Baxter literally bumps into Dylan. Kind, funny, and not-too-shabby in the looks department, Dylan soon wins Ellie and Jake over, and Ellie dares to dream of a happy ending at last.

But as the snow starts to fall and Christmas approaches, Ellie realises time is running out for them. Dylan clearly has a secret that may ruin their happiness, Baxter's home is in jeopardy, and she has no way of making Jake's wishes come true.

Must Ellie give up on her dreams, or can Baxter lead her back to happiness?

Light the fire, switch on those Christmas tree lights, curl up with a hot chocolate, and enjoy this heart-warming festive story of love, home, and second chances.

Christmas with Cary

You never forget your first love.

Molly's spent every Christmas she can remember surrounded by her family. But this year is different. This year, Molly's all alone in a strange town. She's left her family behind, and she's not sure where she can call home any longer. All Molly has with her are a few clothes in a suitcase, and a collection of her old friend's Cary Grant films.

Except, there's one more thing she's brought along - the whole reason for her Christmas visit. In her possession is a small, crumpled piece of paper, and on it is written the address of the love of her life.

Molly and Cary have had many chances over the years, but somehow life kept getting in the way and they always ended up apart once more. Yet Molly has never forgotten the first man she gave her heart to, and now she has one last chance to win him back.

But will Cary welcome her home, or will he tell her what she dreads to hear - that they've had their chance, and it's all too late. That's if she can even find him...

A lovely, festive story about hope, forgiveness, and never giving up on love - however long it takes.

Printed in Dunstable, United Kingdom